DAVID

INSIDE

OUT

Lee Bantle

Christy Ottaviano Books
HENRY HOLT AND COMPANY
New York

I want to gratefully acknowledge my writing teachers, Nancy Kelton and Norma Fox Mazer; my script consultants, Stuart Spencer and Jess Taylor; my agent, Mitchell Waters; my editor, Christy Ottaviano; the Gay/Straight Alliance of Westport High School in Connecticut; and my friends who provided invaluable feedback: Ken Greenwood, Lynn Armentrout, Lou Ann Smith, Cyrus Copeland, Paul Gavriani, Robert Levy, Karla Melvin, Holly Russell, and Janet Pacella Gamza.

Henry Holt and Company, LLC
Publishers since 1866
175 Fifth Avenue
New York, New York 10010
www.HenryHoltKids.com

Henry Holt is a registered trademark of Henry Holt and Company, LLC.
Text copyright © 2009 by Lee Bantle
All rights reserved.
Distributed in Canada by H. B. Fenn and Company Ltd.

Library of Congress Cataloging-in-Publication Data
Bantle, Lee F.
David inside out / Lee Bantle.—1st ed.
p.   cm.
"Christy Ottaviano books."
Summary: At a Minneapolis high school, a cross-country runner tries to deny his sexual feelings for a male teammate.
ISBN-13: 978-0-8050-8122-0 / ISBN-10: 0-8050-8122-4
[1. Homosexuality—Fiction.   2. Self-acceptance—Fiction.
3. Minneapolis (Minn.)—Fiction.]   I. Title.
PZ7.B22945Dav 2009   [Fic]—dc22   2008036779

First edition—2009 / Designed by Laurent Linn
Printed in the United States of America on acid-free paper. ∞

1 3 5 7 9 10 8 6 4 2

For my guys

DAVID

INSIDE

OUT

CHAPTER

ONE

Driving along Minnehaha Parkway on my way to see Kick, I felt like Archie going over to Veronica's. Not because she lived in a massive stone house and I mowed lawns for cash. Or because I was prone to Archie-type screwups. I felt that way because our relationship was two-dimensional.

And that was the test. Could I make it to the third dimension with her?

Rudolphs was packed like always on Saturdays. The buzz ricocheted off pink plaster walls as I squeezed through the rowdy crowd swigging beer in the entry. Eddie was sitting alone in back. "Kick's not here yet?" I asked, sliding my lanky frame into the fake-leather booth.

"In the bathroom—probably stocking up on cheap dispenser condoms," he said, straight-faced.

"Yeah, right."

"Don't be so sure she's not. That girl is in heat." I gave him a look. "Your ears must have been burning," he said.

"You talking about me?"

"Mmhmm. Your sex life."

"What!" I crunched down on an ice cube. "Who brought that up?"

"Kick wants to know why you're so slow."

"She said that?"

"Yeah." Eddie turned the salt shaker on its side and spun it. "Why *are* you so slow? No, really, I want to know."

"Shhh! She's coming," I said.

"There you are, David," Kick said, sliding in next to me. "What took you so long to get here?"

"I got lost."

"That's pathetic." She patted my hand like I was five. "How many times have you been downtown Minneapolis?"

"Downtown!" Eddie replied. "You call this downtown? I can't wait for us to be in New York, Kick."

"New York?" I asked.

Eddie nodded. "We're applying to NYU."

"You are? Both of you?" I looked at Kick.

She nodded and handed me a menu. "I want to go to film school."

Oh, sure, I thought, but didn't say it. "I'm staying here," I said.

"Why? Cut loose a little bit," Eddie said.

The waiter came over. Which was good. Eddie gets on this rant that I'm uptight and who needs it? I ordered the house special: slow-cooked country ribs with corn on the cob, onion rings, and buttermilk rolls.

"Just a large salad for me," Kick said. "Dressing on the side."

I studied her lips as she recounted her adventure to the Mall of America the night before. They were plump, freshly remoistened with gloss. She smiled at me. I sat up straight, brushing the hair out of my eyes. Did she want me to make a move? How?

"My mother is really losing it with me," Kick told us. "I got home a half hour late. Twelve-thirty instead of midnight. Okay, maybe it was quarter to one." She sighed. "Now I have to be home every night by ten. *Including* weekends."

"For how long?" I asked.

"Until further notice."

"Poor baby," Eddie said.

"She's trying to ruin my life. It's envy."

Two platters of ribs arrived, sitting in lakes of barbecue sauce and topped with mounds of golden brown rings. Eddie had both paws covered in sauce in seconds, but I tried to hold back. The waiter set Kick's salad down, and she began poking at it, looking at our plates longingly. I speared her a perfect ring. After cutting off the breading, she ate it slowly, savoring each nibble. I don't know why she didn't eat more. So what if she was chubby.

As Eddie and I gorged, I let my knee brush against hers. She reached down and held it there. My heart sped up. Were we moving into a new dimension? Because you don't hold people's legs under the table if you're just friends.

"You look cute tonight," she said to me.

"I do?"

"*Please*," Eddie interrupted, reaching for another half ear of corn. "I'm eating."

Kick laughed and took her hand off my leg. Was I supposed to touch her knee now? I wiped my fingers on a wet-nap in preparation. Should I just drop my hand on her? Were you supposed to squeeze? As I reached for her leg, Kick's leather bag started squawking like a chicken. "What's that?" I asked, pulling my hand back.

She took out her cell phone and answered it. "My mother," she mouthed. It was after 10:00.

"The depressing thing," Kick said, standing up, "is that she thinks I'm out having sex." She threw up her arms. "I don't even have a boyfriend." Kick looked at Eddie and then me. "But maybe that will change." She dropped a ten on the table, stole an onion ring from my plate, and disappeared into the crowd.

CHAPTER

TWO

As I drove Eddie home from Rudolphs, he made me turn on the interior light to show the letter he got from Stephanie Bond, the author of *Too Hot to Sleep*. I made fun of him when he first wrote to Barbara Taylor Bradford. Until he got a reply. Now we both write letters. To the *great* romance novelists. But you can't send a fan letter unless you truly love the book. That point is sacrosanct with us.

"So what did Ms. Bond have to say?" I asked, backing out of the parking lot. The spotlit cathedral dome shone in the rear window, with the sparkling lights of downtown just beyond.

"Dear Eddie," he read. "Ohhh, she's already calling me 'dear.' I think I'm in love."

"Keep reading."

"No, I can't. I can't share another word." He pulled the letter to his chest and held it there. "It's private between Steph and me."

"Steph?" I said, turning onto Franklin and driving under the freeway overpass. "Eddie, you need help. I'm thinking a residential program."

"You're just jealous," he taunted, poking me with the envelope as we cruised through the "dangerous" part of South Minneapolis.

When he moved into my neighborhood Eddie was ten. I watched him build a fort on the overgrown lot down by Raftegler's Ravine. Cutting away saplings and flattening the tall grass into a comfy bed, Eddie made a secret hideaway. We sat in there that summer reading comics, eating roasted cashews, and spying on people going by on the sidewalk. Sometimes I made loud farting noises with my armpit, until Eddie told me I was embarrassing him.

Now we're both at Whitman. Each year they give scholarships to a few "local" students who live within walking distance of the academy. Which is the only way either of us could go, since the tuition is mucho dinero.

I turned onto Nicollet Avenue and drove past the restaurants and wine bars, with fashionably dressed smokers out front. Then the street grew residential, and I reached Eddie's block. As I turned the corner, the headlights caught two boys TP-ing the neighbor's house. The imps stood frozen in the high beams, then fled, dropping their rolls as they ran.

"Amateurs," Eddie said, climbing out of the car. The headlights illuminated his small, wiry frame and jet-black hair as he picked up a roll and gave it an underhand toss. Looping high over the branches of his neighbor's maple tree, the roll then plopped to the ground. Outside lights on the house flashed on. Racing for his backyard, Eddie disappeared into the dark. I hit the gas, feeling the old thrill of almost getting caught.

On the way home, I detoured to Lake of the Isles. I got out of the car and walked down to the water, past the "City of Lakes" sign. Shining out the windows of the comfortable brick houses snaking along the shoreline was the yellow hue of good lighting. My warm breath escaped into the chill late-September air as I tried to imagine kissing Kick. Slowly, like they do in romance novels. I closed my eyes to conjure her image: braces-perfect smile, round cheeks, curly dark hair. Why couldn't I feel her lips?

A cold gust of wind licked the back of my neck. Shivering, I ran to the car.

Mom was still up when I got home. She followed me into my small upstairs room, wearing the pink terry-cloth robe I got her for Christmas. I pulled off my earphones.

"So, how are Kick and Eddie? Did you have a good time?"

"Mmhmm. We went to Rudolphs."

"Did you have enough money?"

"Yeah." I hate when Mom worries about that. She gives me more than she should. You don't make much money teaching English at the University of Minnesota. I set my iPod down on the dresser and she picked it up. "Who do you listen to on this?"

"Right now? The Supremes."

"That's funny."

"What's funny about it?"

"We danced to them in college."

"Mom, stop!"

"What?"

"The thought of you . . ."

She laughed and tried to pull me into a dance. I jerked my arms away, leaving Mom to do a boogie of her own creation. Horrifying. "Mother!"

"See? I was pretty good."

"On *American Bandstand,* circa 1950."

"I'm not that old." She looked out the window. "You know who was a good dancer—your father."

"Really?" I loved hearing new things about him.

"We had dance parties at the house before you were born."

"And he was good?" That didn't fit my image of Dad.

"Well, I thought so." Mom missed him. I knew that because there were pictures of him all over her room. I was only five when he died, so I hardly remember. But she never got over him.

I stood up to dance with her. She took my arm and twirled underneath it. And then she brushed my head. "You need a haircut."

Suddenly I was twelve years old. "No, I don't."

"This weekend," she said firmly, heading off to bed.

My mom can be confusing without even trying. If I tell her I *have* to do something because *everyone* is doing it, she says *just be yourself.* She says people respect that. But what if you send fan mail to romance writers? And get teary-eyed at chick flicks? What if you still get spooked during thunderstorms? These are not things you want to share with others. Being yourself might make people reject you. People you desperately care about. Being yourself only works if you're basically cool. Which I'm not.

There's another problem with Mom's advice. How can you be yourself if you don't know who that is?

CHAPTER

THREE

We did sprints for the whole workout Monday. Coach was sadistic with his whistle. We were all dragging as we headed back to school.

I dropped onto the bench in front of my locker, breathing in the sharp smell of fresh sweat. Maybe I was too exhausted to have to worry about anything today. I could hear the clicking of combination locks. Sean and Parker, the other two juniors on cross-country, undressed on either side of me. Like gods. Sean Icelandic and Parker Grecian. I kept my eyes closed, head bent to the floor.

"Who's got shampoo?" Sean called out.

"Here," Parker said. A bottle whizzed by my head.

"This shit's for dandruff," Sean said. The bottle whipped back past me. "C'mon, Dahlgren, don't you have any?"

I opened my eyes and watched Sean tug off his running pants. My gaze strayed down before I forced it back to his face. "Hold on," I said hoarsely, as I found shampoo and handed it to him.

He took the bottle and headed off. No way I was following. Not after what happened on the canoe trip. Starting to dress, I heard Coach McIntyre boom at me: "Get in there, Dahlgren! You smell." Delaying as long as I could, I raced into the cream-and-black-tiled shower room, after everyone was out. Safe inside, I let the hot stream of water massage my tired body.

Toweling off, I heard Parker shout out "Tonelli's!" I rushed to get dry, but they were gone by the time I finished. The shampoo I had given Sean was sitting in a soapy puddle on the long bench in front of my locker.

I was standing in our small grassy front yard, thinking it needed one more mow, when my cell rang. I flipped it open.

"Guess what," Kick said. "My parents are gone next weekend."

"Oh, yeah?"

"They made me swear I wouldn't have anyone over." She lowered her voice so that it was almost a whisper. "So I'm keeping it small. Mona, Eddie, you, and me. And maybe Kristy and Alicia. Can you come?"

"Sure."

"Don't say a word," Kick told me before hanging up. "I'll be in lockdown till Christmas if they find out."

I stared at my reflection in the window, pushing my sandy-brown hair behind each ear. Was this the night Kick and I would finally kiss?

・・・

I got to the locker room first on Friday and changed for our meet against Franklin. We were the better team on paper, but their runners could surprise you. The rest of the team filtered in, chattering with nervous energy.

I stood quietly at the end of my locker row, waiting for everyone to get ready instead of going to the field to loosen up. Out of the corner of my eye, I watched Sean and Parker change. I spun away from them, rushed through the door and into the school yard. God! Now I was loitering in locker rooms.

My right foot twitched like it always did as we lined up at the start of the race on the Hiawatha Golf Course. BANG! I leapt into motion. Runners from Whitman and Franklin, spaced across the whole fairway, bounded onto the lawn. My feet drove down into the thick sod harder and faster. I started to pull ahead of the pack. I couldn't believe it. Sean and Parker ran behind. Everyone was behind.

"TURTLE!" Parker shouted. Team code for "Slow and steady wins the race."

But I was not going to slow up now. I ground down on my molars and pushed harder. At 2,500 meters the course turned back on itself. As I rounded the turn, Coach shouted my time. My best ever. "Ease up!" he called.

It didn't matter what anyone said. I couldn't stop now. I would show them. Doubling back, I saw the oncoming mass of sinewy legs pumping down onto the soft earth. They would never catch me. It felt like I could run forever. Until the last 500 meters. When my legs went mushy. John, our captain, raced by me with two runners from Franklin, followed by Parker and Sean. Push! Push! Others whizzed by. I was a 100 meters out, dying. Runners flew by. Even sophomores I always beat. I crossed the finish in eleventh, gasping. We got kicked by our big rival.

The locker room was dead. None of the usual cutting up. I stalled again, sitting in front of my locker, eyes closed. "Hey, Dahlgren," Parker said. "Wake up." I looked at him pulling off his sweat-stained red jersey. "What was your problem today?"

"I don't know."

"Didn't you hear me yell 'turtle'?"

I shrugged. What could I say? Parker slammed the door of his locker and headed for the shower.

"I'd hate to be you right now," Sean said. "I really would." He patted my shoulder as he stepped by.

Leaving school, I walked past John, the captain, hanging my head.

"Don't worry," he said, putting his arm around my shoulder. "You'll do okay next time, man."

"Thanks," I said. "I hope so."

At home that night, I kicked the elm tree on our boulevard so hard the bark chipped off. I knew better than to go out too fast. What was I trying to prove?

Mom saw me out there. I came in the back door and hung my jacket. "What's wrong?" she asked.

"Nothing."

"Yes, there is."

I slumped into a chair at the kitchen table. "I lost the meet for us tonight."

"You did?"

"Yeah, I was eleventh. Worst time in a month."

"What happened?" she asked, scraping some chopped garlic into a soup pot.

"I choked."

"How much off were you?"

"Half a minute."

"Well, that happens. Eleventh isn't so bad." She drizzled the garlic with olive oil and turned on the heat.

"That's not what the team thinks."

"Oh?"

"Parker yelled at me."

"He shouldn't do that."

"Why? I deserve it."

"Hasn't Parker ever had an off day?"

"No."

"Well, he will. And I hope you'll be loyal to him."

Mom poured three cans of tomato sauce into the pot.

"What are you cooking?" I asked. The cooking garlic made the kitchen smell sweet.

"Spaghetti sauce. Should I throw in some browned sausage?"

"Yes. I'm starving." At least there was food. And Mom. To make me feel better when things went south.

CHAPTER

FOUR

I stalled as long as I could, inspecting disposable razors, shaving cream, cologne. "You buy them," I whispered to Kick. Condoms.

She slipped her arm through mine and tugged me to the counter. The beehive-hairdo lady was there. The kabuki makeup on her face traveled down her neck to the cleavage you *really* didn't want to think about, let alone see.

"Whaddya need, kiddo?" she asked. Cheerfully intense.

"Uh . . . a box of condoms," I mumbled.

"What kind ya want?" She waved at the glass shelves behind her.

"Trojans," I said.

"Ribbed, Ultra Thin, lubricated or non?" she asked. It was like ordering a burger. With fries.

Lord, I wanted to get out of there. "Ribbed, non—"

"Get me some Ultra Thins," Kick whispered, pulling a ten out of her jeans and stuffing it in my hand. Great, make it sneaky and even more incriminating.

I gave her a sideways glance. "And a box of Ultra Thins," I told the lady. My voice, all on its own, decided to jump an octave on the word "thins."

"Hey, Dahlgren!" I turned. Sean! He and Parker were coming toward us with a six-pack of Mountain Dew and a jumbo bag of cashews. Sean looked so handsome, tall and lanky, his blond hair spilling over the collar of a suede jacket. His face had cleared up a lot lately.

After the squeaked-out "thins" I was afraid to talk. I tried to sneak the condoms into my jacket pocket, but they flopped out and hit the floor. Parker nudged Sean and they laughed. I bent down, grabbed the box, and jammed it into my jeans.

"See you," I said, grabbing my change. As we rushed away, I looked over my shoulder. Sean winked and licked his lips in a very sexy way. I suddenly wanted to linger.

Back at Kick's, revenge time. We sprawled on the floor of the den, dim in candlelight, the sound system cranking. My turn to deal. Who would the Queen of Hearts victimize next? I prayed for Eddie. My dare was all ready. Send a letter to Stephanie Bond telling her not that he loved her book, but that he loved *her*. Madly. The deck grew smaller as the cards went round and round. Kick, Mona, Eddie, Alicia, and Kristy. And then it landed. The momentous queen. On Eddie. Yes! "Truth," I demanded, "or dare?"

Eddie played up the drama all he could, one hand on his chest. "Truth," he declared with bravado.

"You always take that," I cried.

"So? I have no secrets."

"So, you're chicken."

Mona's face lit up and she laughed. "I've got one for him. If you *had* to pick someone in this room to make love with, who would it be?"

"That's not fair."

"Here's your dare, then," I jumped in.

"All right, fine," he said. "But I'm not going to lie." He looked slowly around the circle at Kick, Mona, Kristy, Alicia, and then back at each of them again.

"We're waiting," Mona said.

"David," he announced.

"What!" Alicia and Kristy exclaimed at the same time.

Kick and Mona exchanged a glance, and everyone grew quiet. I didn't know what to think.

"Oh my God!" Kick screamed, jumping up. "The garage door. My parents are home." She started throwing our coats at us. "Out the back," she whispered. "Hurry." As if that could ever work. Our cars were in front of the house. She fumbled for her bag and then pressed the box of condoms into my hand. "Take them!" We fled out the kitchen door as Kick stuffed pop cans and half-eaten bags of chips into the trash.

Her parents were waiting for us out front. They checked if we'd been drinking and let us go. Kick, on the other hand . . .

I was nervous driving home that night through the ritzy neighborhood of Kenwood, where Kick lived. Eddie sat next to me, unusually quiet.

"Why did you say *me*?" I finally asked him.

"I wasn't going to say a girl. You were the only guy there."

"Huh?"

"That's right. I'm gay. Surprised?"

I looked over at him. "Why are you telling me?"

"I'm telling everyone."

"Well, leave me out of it."

Eddie turned the radio down. "Is that all you can say? You're my best friend."

"We're friends, Eddie, not best friends."

"Right, I remember. You don't believe in 'best friends.'" Eddie made little quote marks with his fingers. I reached his house and pulled over.

"So? . . ." He looked at me intently. I shrugged. "Oh, man." He opened the door and climbed out. "I hate you."

Out in the yard that night, the air felt mild. I dropped down on my back in the dewy grass and stared up. The stars were scattered through the sky like spilled salt. What did Eddie mean by picking me tonight? More important, why did Sean look at me the way he did?

I thought back to those early-morning runs along Minnehaha Parkway with the team. The only sounds were the robins, the creek gurgling, and, when I was lucky, Sean's steady breathing moving alongside me. As I stared upward, I pretended that I was beside him now, our heads close, his silky hair brushing my face. I'd slide my fingers into his, feeling the solidness of his hand.

CHAPTER

FIVE

Next morning, I woke to the sound of the garage door lifting. I flung the covers back and leapt out of bed. Mom was on her way to church. She was picking up Grandma! Where were the condoms?

I ran to my dresser. Yanked out the drawers. Not there. I brought them in from the car, didn't I? The backyard. I had been lying in the grass last night. I bounded down the stairs and raced out the kitchen door in my boxers. Mrs. Timothy peered at me from her garden. I didn't care. I dove onto the lawn and groped the grass.

I rushed out to the garage. Retraced every step I took. I tore my bed apart. Looked in all my pants pockets. Nowhere.

I tried Eddie's cell but got his recording. So I called his landline. His mother answered and gave him the phone.

"Is your mom standing right there?" I asked.

"Uh-huh."

"You know the . . . ah . . . the . . . items I purchased last night?"

"Uh-huh."

"Did you take them? Please say you did."

"No."

"You left them in the car?"

"On the front seat," he said. He laughed and hung up on me.

I stood holding the phone. Maybe they were hidden by the seat belt. But Grandma always wore her seat belt! I fell onto my bed. If I told Mom the truth when she asked (and I knew she'd ask!), it would look like I was lying. I should make Kick call my mother and explain the whole thing.

I was eating Tasteeos with raisins and milk when Mom got back from church. "Hi," I managed to say, half-standing up. She opened her purse, took out the red box of Trojans, and tossed it on the kitchen table. "I believe these are yours," she said pointedly.

I gulped. "Don't jump to conclusions."

"What do you expect me to think?" She sat down next to me at the gray Formica table. "You should have gone to church with me today." I could feel my ears turning red. "David . . ."

"What?"

"Why do you have these?"

"I don't want to talk about this."

She gave me a firm look. "I want to know. Are you having sex?"

God, I was dying. "It's none of your business."

"Yes, it is."

"Mom, drop it."

"I will. As soon as you talk to me."

"No, we're done." I grabbed the condoms and bounded up the stairs, mortified.

"DAVID!" she called after me.

Up in my room, I lay down on the floor, put on my headphones, and cranked the music. After a few minutes I felt her presence. What did she want now? I lifted the headphone from one ear.

"I'm glad you're using protection," she said quietly and then disappeared from my room.

I had just finished changing on Monday when Sean and Parker strolled into the locker room. "Hey, hey, how was it?" Parker called to me. He came over and started boxing my shoulder. "What a man."

I smiled sheepishly and leaned down over my shoes. They were already tied, but I undid them and started over.

Parker bent his face near my ear. "How many times did you nail her?" he asked.

"Get lost," I said, pushing him away. He and Sean both laughed.

The team did speed work in Lake Nokomis, basking in the warm September sun as our feet froze in the icy water. We must have been a sight to the joggers on the grassy boulevard around the lake, sweeping our legs through the knee-deep water to strengthen our quads.

Coach McIntyre was ready with towels on the beach as the team splashed out of the lake. We sat in the sand, getting our socks and shoes back on, but no resting was allowed. As Coach sent everyone off for distance work, he grabbed my shoulder. "You're running timed miles," he growled. "Until you feel the right pace."

When we were done, I got a ride back to school in Coach's car. "Everything all right at home?" he asked as we drove past rows of pointed stucco houses.

I nodded. "Yeah, fine."

"Good." He cracked his window. "Can I give you a piece of advice?"

"Okay."

"Get to know yourself better."

I looked surprised.

"That's the most important part of high school," he said. "For all of you."

I contemplated that for the rest of the drive. Reaching the school parking lot, we unloaded the towels and went inside.

No one had returned by the time I'd showered and dressed.

As I cut across the grass on my way home, I ran into Sean jogging back toward school, the first of the team to return. He stopped. "Hey, Dahlgren."

He was smiling at me. "When did you get to be such a stud?"

I rolled my eyes. He reached for my stomach and started tickling.

"Stop!" I said, grabbing his arm.

He started on me with the other hand. I grabbed that arm and pulled him. He fell against me. And then he jumped away when the rest of the team came jogging around the corner.

"Don't worry, I won't tell anyone about you," he said, heading for the shower.

Won't tell anyone what?

CHAPTER

SIX

Invisible arrows, dipped in nausea and dread, shot into my chest as I jumped in place on the starting line. My heart vibrated like a rabbit's. Please, please, God, don't let me choke again.

The starter moved into position, and I pulled off my sweats. The brisk wind raised bumps on my legs. "I'll pace you," Sean said, falling into place next to me.

I looked over at him, amazed. "Thanks." Was he worried about me? Or just about winning the most important meet of the year? Against Breck for first.

"Set!" yelled the starter. The gun rang out, and we leapt forward. I stayed a half stride behind Sean. At 1,500 meters, John safely held the lead, then came Parker and a runner from Breck. Sean and I followed in the middle of a pack. Why didn't he break out? I could hear grunts and the pounding breath of runners on all sides of me. I wanted out of this big group.

But Sean just hung back, content to be part of the mob. I stayed close to him, imagining that it was just the two of us running. I found his breath and meditated on it. We ran and ran. That's when it came over me—runner's bliss. I didn't have to work anymore. The muscles in my legs seemed to disappear, and I moved across the course like a ghost, weightless, able to run forever. No care in the world could touch me.

With 300 meters to go, Sean sped up. We passed two sophomores on our team. As he went faster and faster, I began to feel the weight of my legs again. We passed three Breck runners. The urge to cave in pulled at my body, but I pushed forward, never letting Sean get more than a stride ahead. In the last fifty meters, my muscles ached for oxygen. I thought I was going to fall back. But I saw Sean raising his arms and flying in behind Parker and John. Lunging for him, I finished a step behind.

I crashed to the grass, gulping air. Sean came over to me. A trail of snot ran from his nose. "Get up," he said. "Walk." As I pushed off the ground, he grabbed my hand and pulled me up. Tears rushed to my eyes.

John and Parker mobbed us. We all danced and hugged. Standing in the circle of their arms, Sean's shoulder pressing into my chest, I laughed and shouted, "We won!"

I was wiped out when I finally got in the shower. I stood under the spray, hot as I could stand it. I could hear the team out in the locker room, whipping towels and sliding across the wet floor. I raced to get done. When I got back to my locker, Sean was still standing in his briefs. I let myself glance at him for two seconds, holding the towel tightly around me. Then I whipped open my locker and jumped into my pants.

"Hey, David," he said as I dressed. David. He called me David. "You want to get pizza?"

Did I want to?

The sky, faded rose and blue like a tie-dyed shirt, was luminous as we pushed open the big double doors at the front of Whitman. I scrambled down the grooved marble steps, John and Parker ahead, Sean by my side.

CHAPTER

SEVEN

We sat so close I could feel the heat radiating from Sean's body under the folds of the green-checked tablecloth. My arm hairs stood on end. John filled our glasses from the pitcher on the table; Tonelli's celery soda could have been nectar of the gods.

After we ordered, Parker and John went over to the jukebox and began picking songs.

"There's something I have to ask you," Sean said after they left the table.

I sat up in my chair. "Ask me. Anything."

"Not here." He nodded at Parker and John approaching the table. If I'd had a ray gun, they would've both been wisps of smoke. "Let's go for a bike ride."

"When? Tonight?"

"No," Sean said, looking out the window at the darkness. "This weekend. Okay?"

I nodded. What did he have to ask me? Could it possibly be that he had feelings like mine?

I believe in miracles, I told myself. I do. I do. I do.

. . .

I was playing Jezzball on the computer in Kick's den. She started massaging my shoulders and neck.

"I have to leave in a half hour," she said.

"Thought you were grounded."

"I'm allowed to go to tutoring."

"Really? *You're* failing something?"

Kick dug her fingers into my neck. "No. I'm helping Keisha get ready for her fourth-grade reading test."

"You're a good person, aren't you?"

"When I'm not naughty."

"Yeah?"

"Look." Kick tugged her jeans down on one side, and there was a blood-red rose tattooed on her hip.

"Is that permanent?"

"Uh-huh. Isn't it sexy?"

"Yeah, I guess."

"You don't like it?"

"No, I do. It's cool."

"You're the only guy who gets to see it. Which makes you special."

I beamed at her. Then I got shy. "What's this?" I asked, glancing down at the leather book with silver on the cover in the shape of a goblet.

"My bat mitzvah album," Kick said, picking it up from the desk.

I grabbed it. "Let me see."

"No." She pulled it away. "I'm too fat."

"Come on."

"Oh, all right."

We sat down on the couch next to each other, and she put the album in my lap. It was funny to see her real name—Katherine Shapiro—written out. Nobody called her that. Not even the teachers at school. Kick started flipping through the album, leaning forward, one arm resting on my knee. Her black hair fell against her white cashmere sweater, and I could smell the herbal shampoo she used. I reached up and touched it. She looked back at me, smiling. And at that moment I felt a wonderful, hopeful tingling down there where it counts, where you can't fake it, even if you really, really want to.

CHAPTER

EIGHT

I stayed home all weekend waiting for Sean to call. Mom left Sunday after church. She took Grandma down to the Mayo Clinic. More tests for her irregular heartbeat. I moved from chair to chair that afternoon reading *Surrender My Love*.

Ding-dong. I went to the front door. It was Eddie, with his golden retriever, Shirley.

"Can we hang out here?" he asked.

The dog started licking my hands. "Well . . ." How could I say no?

"My dad's back, and he's in one of his rages."

Eddie's dad was an NRA member. You knew from all the bumper stickers on his truck. He and his buddies had a "hunting lodge" in North Dakota. He took Eddie and me ice fishing there once. It was ten below zero, and we were all sitting with lines hanging down into this hole in the ice. Eddie lasted about ten minutes before he went to the truck and turned on the heater. I stayed out there with his dad until my hands were blue. I don't know why, maybe to avoid getting judged along with Eddie. When we finally wound our line in, he told me that Eddie was a girlie boy, but maybe someday I'd be a man.

"You want to go up to my bookcase and pick something out?" I offered, hugging Shirley, who licked my face.

"Yeah." Eddie tore up the stairs. "How is Barbara Freethy?" he called down to me.

"Great."

"*Some Kind of Wonderful* or *One True Love*?"

"*Wonderful* is my favorite."

Eddie came bounding down the stairs, studying the back cover.

We were sitting in the living room, reading our romances, when my cell finally rang. At last! "Bye, Eddie," I said, opening the phone. "Hello," I said hopefully.

Eddie moved right next to me. "Who is it?" he asked.

"Get out of here." I pushed him toward the door. "It's my uncle Mark."

"See ya," Eddie called as he headed for the door. "Come on, Shirley."

Two hours later, slouched in the overstuffed chair in the living room, I admitted to myself Sean wasn't going to call. Why did it make me feel so bad, so embarrassed? My mind drifted back to the trip to the Boundary Waters this past summer. That's where it started.

We were all the way to the Minnesota-Canada border, the whole cross-country team, in the wilderness. After canoeing all day, we stopped at a campsite with sheer cliffs perfect for jumping into the water. The team took turns going airborne. Guys clambered up the cliffs in their wet skivvies to jump, and I couldn't take my eyes off them as I treaded water below. That's when it happened. Staring at Sean as he bounced up and down getting ready to jump, I felt myself go hard. I couldn't get out of the water for almost twenty minutes.

Sitting in the dusk weeks later, thinking about that moment, I realized it had happened again. What was it about Sean? I had to see him. I had to be with him.

I looked up his number in the phone book. I'd never called him before, but why couldn't I? His mother answered. "Who's this?" she asked, and I gave my name.

Sean picked up. "Thought we were going biking," I reminded him.

"Oh, yeah, sorry," he said. "My cousins came over. We're watching movies."

"Didn't you want to ask me something?" I said.

"Well, yeah. . . ."

"What?"

"Um, well, you see the team's evenly split. Some for Parker, some for me. Your vote decides who'll be the next captain."

"That's all you wanted?" He was grubbing for votes.

"Why? You didn't want to be captain, did you?" Sean asked.

"No." I didn't hope for things I knew I wouldn't get.

"So, wouldn't you rather have me than Parker?"

"Of course. I'm just surprised you thought you had to ask."

"My dad *really* wants me to be captain."

"Fine, then."

"Thanks. See you at practice tomorrow."

What a dick he was! I threw myself back into the chair. Sitting there, I couldn't get Sean out of my mind. I reached one hand under my shirt and painted my chest with a finger. Alive with sensation, my body jumped at the slightest touch. I slid my hand down, and imagined him standing in front of me. I moved to the floor, sprawling out on my back, fantasizing. Never before had I thought about Sean like this. Drinking in the full frontal view of him, I knew what I wanted and I went for it. My muscles tensed. I sucked in a breath as a powerful shudder seized my body. And then a second one. A third. A fourth. God, the ferocity of it. I fell back, woozy.

Then I saw the spot on the rug. What had I done? I got paper towels, wet them, and scrubbed at the carpet. I took the whole wet glob upstairs and flushed it down the toilet, catching my reflection in the mirror. My eyes were blazing. I saw my mother's lipstick sitting out on the counter. I pulled off the top, wound it out, and stabbed at my lips. I was a girlie boy too. Trying to force back tears, I jammed my eyes shut, but it was no use. I went into my room and fell onto the bed. The tears streamed down across my caked lips, washing into the pillow.

I don't know how long I lay there. An hour? At some point, I couldn't stand the chalky taste of the lipstick anymore. I got up, washed my face and lips, and rinsed with mouthwash.

Then I sat at the top of the staircase in the dark, listening to the branches of our spindly poplar tree whipping against the window. I shivered.

This wasn't me. It couldn't be. Not gay. Anything but that. I grabbed a notepad and a pen and started writing:

1. Do not look at male bodies! Especially Sean's. Practice mind control. Think of Halle Berry instead.

I opened the drawer, found a fat rubber band, and put it on my wrist. Then I snapped it. That would do the trick.

2. No more solo sex. Unless you think about girls.
3. Hang out more with real men. Like Parker. Bonus points if Eddie's dad takes you fishing again.
4. Fall in love with a girl.

I never really got close with Alice Chamberlain last summer. I thought she was pretty. We both liked biking. But by summer's end it had fizzled. We didn't even make out. I had to change that dynamic, to become more passionate. I had to fall in love. Or at least have sex.

After reading the list over and over until it was memorized, I tore it into dozens of tiny pieces. I put half of them inside a paper bag in my wastebasket and then went downstairs and put the rest inside a cereal box in the trash. Up in bed, pillowcase changed, teeth scrubbed, things felt better. I had a plan to save myself.

CHAPTER

NINE

A wall of magazines stood before me. I grabbed *Car and Driver* and *Iron Man*. Then I saw *Guns & Ammo*. I groaned and picked up a copy.

Playboy was at the top of the rack. How old did you have to be to buy it? I risked it and got away with it. Maybe because I had bought gas and paid with a credit card.

Mom was at the kitchen table grading her students' essays when I came home. "What did you buy?" she asked, seeing my bag.

"Just some magazines."

"Shouldn't you be doing your homework instead of reading magazines?"

"I'm keeping up."

"I want you to do more than keep up."

"Don't worry."

"What are you studying in English?"

"German literature."

"I'll help you if you need it."

"I'm fine." English was my best subject. Mr. Detweiler took a shine to me in that class.

I shot upstairs. That night, I studied physics with the radio cranking. Then it was into bed with the magazines. I began looking at the pictures on the glossy covers. A black Ferrari convertible. A stacked redhead showing her cleavage. A muscle-bound guy pressing weights. What a chest! I flipped open that one. The whole magazine was filled with shirtless guys. I felt a stirring. What was I doing with this? I flung it down.

I opened *Playboy* to the centerfold. Miss October was voluptuous. I wouldn't mind feeling up her big, soft breasts. On the next page, she was posed with her legs spread. I tried to imagine how soft it must be inside there in an attempt to get aroused. But it was no use, so I grabbed for *Car and Driver*.

The image of Sean undressing came to me. I pushed it away and turned to an article about the souped-up power in the new fall models from Germany. Instead of cars, I envisioned very tall, chisel-jawed blond guys, all named Karl. I fell asleep, pages in hand, wondering how many articles on V6 engines I would have to read before I stopped having a thing for guys. I'd probably end up going blind either way.

The next day I noticed a dark-haired woman looking out the window of Parker's house as I headed up his walk. I knew she was watching me.

I rang the bell and waited, squishing my fingers into the spiral binding of my history notebook. Don't blow it! I cautioned myself, figuring Sean and Parker had asked me to study with them on a trial basis.

The woman who had been watching opened the heavy wooden door. "Hello," she said in a low, raspy voice, gesturing for me to come in. "I haven't met *you* before, have I?"

"David Dahlgren," I said, forcing myself not to stare at her.

Her gaze worked me up and down and came back to my face. "Hello, David," she said, taking my hand. "Call me Charlotte."

"Is Parker here?" I asked, wondering when she was going to let go of my fingers.

She nodded, and led me through the front hallway. "Are you hungry? Want to see what you're having for dinner?"

What could I say? We walked past a dozen gleaming copper pots hanging over a white marble island. She opened the oven to show me two oblong birds browning, crackling, and popping in the heat. I could smell the rich juices dripping out of them. "Looks good," I said, suddenly hungry.

She closed the oven, turned, and stared at me. "You like to eat, don't you?" I nodded. Didn't everyone? I sure wished she would get Parker.

"Mom!" Thank goodness, Parker found us in the kitchen. "Would you tell me when my friends get here?" Did I hear that right? He used the word "friend." "Come on." Parker led me to the staircase. The double-padded carpeting sunk with each step. I checked my shoes to be sure they were clean. "Sorry you got kidnapped," he said.

Parker's basement was not like ours, with a big furnace and cement floor. It had a poolroom, with cues, bridges, and chalk, a study with floor-to-ceiling carved wooden bookshelves, and a family room filled with leather furniture, an enormous TV, and a bar.

"Hey, Dahlgren," Sean greeted me as he leaned back on two legs of a bar stool, looking good in his forest-green sweater and khaki slacks. I snapped the rubber band on my wrist.

Parker took cans of Mountain Dew out of the little refrigerator behind the bar and gave us each one. "Hey, did you guys see Jenny Melcher today?"

Sean rolled his eyes at me. "Parker's totally obsessed."

"You could see her nipples through that leotard thing," Parker said.

"So you stared at her chest all day?" Sean asked.

"No!" Parker aimed his soda at Sean's face as he popped the lid. "You think I should call her?"

"Why not?" I asked.

Sean opened his notebook. "Okay, shut up, Parker. Let's get some work done."

Parker reached out his hands as if he were squeezing Melcher's breasts. "I'd love to have her."

Sean looked up at him skeptically. "Would you go beat off or something?" He started laughing and I did too.

Parker gave Sean a dirty look. "Shut up, you preppy fag." Then he looked at me. "You're both pretty faggy."

I felt my face go red, and buried it in my notes. Why should it bother me? I wasn't going to be like that. I was going to be like him.

"Who was the first emperor of Rome?" I called out.

"Julius Caesar," Parker replied, as if it was obvious.

"Augustus," Sean said. They let me quiz them on Roman history until Parker's mother brought down dinner. She smiled while handing over a plate loaded with sliced dark morsels, cranberries, and mashed potatoes drizzled with gravy. I forked a piece of the roasted meat into my mouth.

"How's the duck?" Parker's mom asked. So that's what it was. She looked at me expectantly.

"Mmmmm, delicious."

"Okay, Mom, we've got to get back to work."

"There's dessert too," she called as she climbed the stairs. "Tarte tatin."

"What's that?" I asked.

Parker looked at Sean. "See, there's at least one fag thing he doesn't know."

Sean just shook his head.

The history midterm the next day asked nothing about the Roman emperors. On two of four essay questions, I was forced to be extremely creative. Afterward, Sean found me in the hallway. "Blew that one out," he said, scowling. "We have to work harder tonight."

"Tonight?"

"Yeah. We've got English tomorrow, don't we?"

He just assumed I was studying with them. That amazed me.

"Where?"

"Parker's house," he replied.

"Hey, can I ask you something?"

"What?"

"Well . . ." I fingered the coins in my pants pocket. "Parker's mother. What's with her?"

Sean laughed. "She got the hots for you?" We reached the staircase. I went down and he went up. "If she asks you to caddie for her, don't do it," he called over the banister. I couldn't see Sean anymore, but I heard his laugh echoing from above.

"Spike it!" I yelled. The ball floated over Mom in perfect position. She jumped. "Ohhhh, Mom!"

She laughed as the ball thudded to earth. "Sorry, hon."

It was Uncle Mark's annual volleyball tournament. Mom, Mark, and I were against his wife, Elaine, and a neighbor couple. A cooler of beer and soda sat next to the net. I took a Michelob watchfully, but no one had a problem with it.

After the rout (our side lost all three games), Elaine served brunch. Bagels and lox with three kinds of cream cheese, spicy red onions, tomatoes, and fruit salad. Mom squeezed in between me and Mark at the table on the porch. "You made some good shots," he said to me.

I nodded. "You did too."

"So what happened to us?"

Mom put her arms around our shoulders. "I happened. I'm the black hole of volleyball skill." She picked up her overstuffed bagel and bit into it. Tomato juice spurted down her chin.

I hugged her, loving the feeling of family.

We made it through exams week. I doubted my grades would be any good. But that didn't bother me so much. You could always pull it out at finals. What I kept thinking about was whether Sean or Parker would call that weekend. With midterms finished, was I over too?

It wasn't until English on Monday that I saw them again. "Listen to this," Parker whispered to us in the hallway after class. "You know who I spent Saturday night with? Jenny Melcher." Parker laughed. "Put your tongues back in your mouths, guys."

"What happened?" Sean asked, brushing his arm against mine. I looked at him out of the corner of my eye, but he was staring at Parker.

"We were at this party together, right," Parker picked up. "Ooh, man, I'm getting whipped up just thinking about it. She let me drive her home. Only I made a little detour."

"Yeah?" Sean encouraged him.

"Let's just say there were a few curves involved before I went into the tunnel."

"You dog," Sean said.

"Nail her for me next time," I blurted out. I expected guffaws from Parker, but he just swaggered off.

"She your type?" Sean asked, studying my face. "She doesn't look much like Parker's mom." Then he grabbed me by the nipple through my shirt and twisted, laughing demoniacally.

CHAPTER

TEN

After school on the second Friday in October, the team crammed into two cars and headed for the regionals. Only the top ten finishers would move on to state. I listened to the flap-slapping of the windshield wipers shunting off the rain as we drove, wondering if anyone would come to see me race. I wanted to win. I wanted us to win. Mostly, I was relieved that the season was ending.

Dozens of runners, most of them still in their bright warm-ups, were spread out across the grass where the course started and ended. Inspecting the grounds, a sponge from the downpour earlier, I imagined what it would be like to take this race. Would leading the pack make me feel okay about myself?

I didn't pay attention to the words Coach called out as he rallied us for the race. But I felt the lift from his booming voice and from the roar we sounded when he finished. We gathered on the crowded starting line. Sean stepped in close to me. I tried not to notice the fuzziness of his leg hair tickling my skin. "Let's show them all," he said very quietly. I nodded.

Two judges reviewed the long line of runners as the starter raised his gun. A cold mist beaded on my face. BANG! I hurled myself forward. More than twenty of us reached the narrowing into the woods together. There was no grass, the earth was a mud pit. As the crush of runners tried to squeeze through, a shoulder dug into my side. It knocked me off stride. I slid into a body in green shorts. We both crashed into the mud.

I plunged my hand into the muck and shoved myself back up. Runners were slipping and falling all around me. I made it through the gap in the trees only to find a long line ahead of me on the wooded path. I couldn't see Sean. He was supposed to pace me!

I clenched my teeth and drove my legs down as hard and fast as I could, brushing at the mud caked on them. Better to risk dying at the end than never catching up. I began to pass runners.

After 1,500 meters, the course shot out of the woods into a long grassy field and then circled back on itself. We had to go through that gap again. I counted eighteen ahead of me at the halfway point. John and Parker ran clustered near the front. Sean stayed just behind the pack. Slowly, I gained on him.

I passed a cluster of runners. Sean was less than thirty meters ahead now. My lungs were straining. The mist had hardened into a cutting rain.

Suddenly, Sean toppled, elbows flying, into the mud pit where I had fallen before. His body thudded, and I heard him groan. "Get up!" I screamed as I hurtled by. Runners charged past him, and he just lay there.

The last hundred yards were a blur. I heard footfalls all

around me. Just before the finish line, I saw Kick. Next to her, under a red-and-white umbrella, was Eddie. "Go!" she screamed. "Go!" I lowered my head and lunged across the finish line—way out of the top ten. I took three more steps and then fell into the grass.

I forced myself up on one knee and then stood. Parker and John were embracing, jumping up and down. They both qualified. Coach came over and clapped his arm around my shoulder. "Strong finish, David. Next year, we'll get you to state."

I saw Kick waving to me. I ran to her and threw my arms around her. "David," Eddie said, "you're getting her all muddy." She clamped on and hugged me back.

Where was Sean? I turned and looked up and down the park. There he was, off by himself, staring blankly. I walked over.

He kicked at the grass, working up a divot with his shoe. I thought there were tears on his face, but with the rain I couldn't be sure.

"You'll still make a good captain," I said.

"Forget it. Parker's got a lock."

After the meet, Parker jumped onto a bench in the locker room, whistled, and told us he'd buy us all pizza at Tonelli's. Everyone went except Sean. What was with him? He wanted to win, but he didn't usually sulk when he lost.

Parker had two bottles of champagne stashed in his trunk. We took turns leaving the table and going out with him to guzzle from the bottle. He had it in an ice bucket. Classy guy.

On my second trip to his car, Parker pulled out the last

half bottle and took a long swig. He handed it to me and then flung his arm around my shoulder. "You're okay, Dahlgren," he said. I raised the heavy dark bottle to my lips, tilted it high, and drank.

"But *that guy* you're friends with. What a fag."

The champagne went down wrong, shot out my nose, and I coughed. Parker dropped his arm and took the bottle, laughing. "Who?" I asked when I stopped choking.

"You know, he was at the race under that pussy umbrella."

"Eddie?"

"Yeah. I heard he pays to smell guys' dirty jocks."

"I doubt it—he doesn't have much money."

"So you give him yours for free, right?" Parker gave me a boozy nudge. "Bet he's got the hots for you, Davey." I shook my head. "I'm just telling you. Keep your butt in the corner when he's around."

My fingers curled into a tight fist in my pants pocket, but I stayed silent. Parker was just drunk.

"Well?" Mom stood in the front hallway. Waiting for a full report.

"I had my best race ever," I said, trying to talk with my lips mostly together to hide the smell of booze.

"Why are you talking like that?" she asked.

"Like what?" I said, enunciating.

"So it was a good day? I'm so glad."

"Coach said I'll go to state next year."

"Oh, David. That's great."

"But Sean fell in the mud. And he didn't place."

"How did he take that?"

"Not well."

"See, everyone has an off day."

She smiled at me, and I basked in her approving glance. Despite the pizza, I suddenly felt ravenous. That's what it was like on race days. "What's for dinner?"

"Stuffed meat loaf."

"What's it stuffed with?"

"Sausage and cheese."

"Yum." I ran off to shower.

Lying in bed that night, I tried to figure out what to do about Eddie. Apparently everyone knew he was gay. He was the only guy that girls consulted on their hair styles. He knew when they were having their periods. And he didn't like sports or cars or anything that I was now into. Maybe it was time for me to branch out.

I wondered what Sean was doing right then. I wished he were sitting next to me on my bed. I could see him with that green sweater on, looking glum. . . .

I started to massage his back to console him. "Oh, that feels
good," he said.

"You like that?"

"Mmhmm." He stretched out on the bed, and I fell onto him. . . .

I snapped the rubber band till my wrist turned red.

I tried to fall asleep, but couldn't. I slipped my hand under the covers. I had to think about a girl. Someone real. *Playboy* didn't work for me.

I conjured Parker's girlfriend, Jenny. She was lying on her bed, naked, waiting for me. It was turning me on some, and then Parker came into the fantasy. I forced myself to switch images. I thought of Mona. But she didn't want me. So that didn't work. My mind started to slip back to Sean. No!

I thought of Mandy Moore. At the golf course. Why? I don't know. I was caddying. She hit her ball into the rough, way back behind a grove of trees. As I looked for it, she followed me into the woods.

"You young stud," she said, like a character out of one of my romance novels. Somehow, this fantasy worked. Unreal. Safe. I didn't care what happened to her, and forgot everything but the sensation under my blanket. I could feel hot breath on my neck, imagined her firm nipple in my mouth. My muscles grew taut . . . ohh, ohhh . . . yeah! My arm fell to my side. I opened my eyes.

Good God! Mandy Moore?

CHAPTER

ELEVEN

As the shrinking days of mid-October gradually gave way, one after another, the wind shifted, swooping down from Canada with blasts so strong you needed to wrap yourself in fleece just to go outside for a breath of air. The leaves on Mrs. Timothy's sugar maples turned gold and red with the dry, cold nights. You couldn't pretend anymore that the wintry days were far away.

The cross-country season had ended. No whistle drills, no sweat, no guarantee of seeing Sean and Parker, except in English. Would they forget about me now? Granted, I hadn't made the best study buddy. We all got C's on the history test.

I sat on our steps in the afternoon sun, watching the maple leaves next door come down. They swirled and flew in the breeze, then dropped onto the lawn.

Mrs. Timothy came out and offered me twenty dollars to rake them all up. Sure, I told her, eager for the money. Crinkly dry leaves caught on the prongs of my bamboo rake as I swept them into a pile. The heap grew larger and larger. When I had them all piled up, I couldn't resist taking a running jump into them. I landed in the cushion of leaves and sprawled back, inhaling their sweet scent.

As I lay there, I heard a car door slam and a voice. "*What* are you doing?" I sat up, leaves clinging to my hair. Sean was staring at me. "Having fun?" he asked.

"Yeah." I sprinkled a few more leaves down on my head.

"Brought back your English notebook," Sean said, thrusting it toward me.

"Oh, thanks." I stood, brushing myself off.

"Did you see Parker working out on the front steps of school today?" Sean asked. "So everyone would see him?"

"He did that?"

"Yeah. Sickening."

"He's a little conceited," I said.

"A little?"

I started raking the leaves back into a pile. Sean watched me. "Go ahead and jump," I said when it was mounded high again.

"Nah."

"Go on. You know you want to." Sean stood immobile. "I'll throw you in if you don't," I said.

"Dare you."

I sprang at him and he started to run around the pile. I chased him and then dove across to tackle him at the waist. We struggled, Sean trying to stay up, while I tried to force him down. Finally we collapsed into the pile, scattering leaves everywhere. Our bodies landed chest to chest, with me on top.

I could feel his lungs rising and falling as he caught his breath. I brushed the leaves out of his hair. Sean shoved my shoulders back and rolled over on top of me, thrusting his hips down into mine. Then he moved up and put one knee on each of my arms, pinning me, his crotch inches from my mouth.

"How do you like that?" he asked.

"Your knees are digging into me."

Sean lifted one knee and then the other to free my arms, but stayed poised over me. "Better?"

"What's going on out there?" Mrs. Timothy called from her stoop.

We both jumped up like the leaves had caught fire. I started raking furiously.

Sean turned. "I better go." He ran down the lawn to his car.

"Wait," I said, but he drove off. I fell back into the leaves, not caring what old Timothy might say, and snapped the band on my wrist twenty times.

I was scarfing down my second freezer chicken potpie Wednesday night, when the phone rang. Mom answered. "It's Eddie."

Why couldn't he go on a long vacation to Africa? I looked at Mom and shrugged. "I'm eating."

"Eddie, can he call you back?"

Mom poured herself another cup of coffee and sat down. "Uncle Mark called. He has two tickets to the Guthrie Theater on Sunday. Do you want to go?"

"What's the show?"

"A Tennessee Williams play."

I speared a little onion with my fork and popped it into my mouth. "Never heard of him."

"You don't know Tennessee Williams?"

I shrugged. "Don't you want to go? You love the Guthrie." I dug a long strip of crust off the edge of the aluminum mini-pie pan and ate it.

"Mark wants to take you."

"Well. Okay." Maybe it would inspire me to start up my journal again. I heard my phone ring and ran upstairs to answer it.

"I got another letter," Eddie crowed. "From Stephanie Bond. I wrote her how much I loved *Our Husband,* and she wrote back again. Can you believe it? I think I'm in love." He sighed.

"Eddie! Snap out of it."

"Oh, you're just jealous. No one's written you back for months."

"I'm not sending out letters anymore."

"Since when?"

"Since a while."

"Well, don't you want to see this one? I'll let you read it. Come over."

"I'm studying."

"Tomorrow then."

"I've got plans tomorrow."

"Doing what?"

"Going out with Sean and Parker, probably."

"Oh. Sure. *If* they call you."

"Eddie, I gotta go." I hung up.

There was a time when Eddie and I were inseparable. A long time ago. Fifth and sixth grade. Everything he did made me laugh. Especially the rude things he said behind our teachers' backs. He wasn't afraid to get into trouble either. Like when he confused World War I and World War II in social studies class and said, "Oh, I really pulled a boner." Everyone broke up and Mr. Cannon made him stay after to write a five-hundred-word essay on war suffering.

He used to come to my house every night after school. Or I went to his. To play with his dog, Shirley, in the backyard or mess around with his chemistry set. Eddie tried for explosions, but usually got snuff-outs. We played Stratego and Risk. I didn't even mind that Eddie posted his victories on the bulletin board next to the furnace.

Then came seventh grade. And the milkshake incident. I rode over to his house on my bike after school. He had gotten this really severe, spiky haircut. "You look like you were struck by lightning," I said.

"As if you had any sense of style," he replied.

"It's pretty freaky," I said.

And suddenly he threw his strawberry malt all over me. It was dripping from my face, my arms, my hair. The guy had no self-control.

He apologized profusely, took me to a Laundromat, and

washed my nylon jacket and shirt. But I told him saying you're sorry is not a cure-all.

Our friendship slackened off. Not completely, we still went to museums and stuff. But in junior high I made new friends.

Then we both got accepted to Whitman on scholarship. I called him the week before school to find out what classes he had. I wanted one friend there. He was half decent on the call. Eddie had grown up some. So I started picking him up, and we walked to school together. We became buds again. He introduced me to Kick and Mona.

I felt bad moving on from him now. But he had other friends. He didn't need me. At least that's what I wanted to believe.

Mom came up after her cable news program was over. "How's your studying coming? Have time for a game of Scrabble?" She had the box in her hand.

"You're on. If you give me a twenty-point head start."

"Since when? No. We both start at zero."

"It's not fair, Mom. You're an English professor."

She laughed and got out the board. I turned the tiles over, knowing I could never beat her. But I loved playing anyway. It was relaxing and took my mind off everything else.

"Do you want to go to New York again this summer?" she asked, drawing her tiles.

"Sure. And stay with Aunt Jennie?"

"Yeah, she said we're welcome."

"Definitely."

"Okay, I'll find out dates from her. Go ahead, you start."

The game went fast. I lost 112 to 168, but it was the first time I cracked a hundred.

"Good job, hon," Mom said as she patted my foot. And then she was off to bed.

As I fell asleep, I thought about the best moment on our last trip to New York. Mom and I were sitting on the edge of the Great Lawn in Central Park. The sunlight filtered down through birch trees. We didn't say anything for a long time, but that's what made it special. Just Mom and me, side by side, listening to a few chirping birds and watching the world go by.

CHAPTER

TWELVE

A white envelope fell to the floor when I opened my locker. I picked it up and read the printed words on the outside: "OPEN WHEN ALONE"

I looked up and down the crowded hallway, slipped the envelope into my pants pocket, and headed to first period. For fifty-five minutes the note steamed in my pocket. When the bell rang, I rushed out the back door and ripped it open.

> Want to get it on with a guy?
> Wear your red jersey on Friday.
> Wait on the steps outside after school.
> I'll meet you.
> DON'T TELL ANYONE!!!
> DON'T SHOW THIS NOTE TO ANYONE!!!
> I am not messing with you.

I read the note straight through three times, then folded it and shoved it deep into my pocket.

In English class, as Detweiler questioned us about the symbolism in Kafka's *Metamorphosis*, I fingered the note. I did a quick turnaround to glance at Sean. Did he send it? More likely it was Parker testing me. Wear that shirt and I was dead. I glanced at Eddie on the other side of the room. Could it be one of his tricks? Or worse. What if he was serious?

I glanced back toward Sean again. He was looking at me! I spun my head around to face forward and sucked in a long breath.

The bell rang, and I moved slowly for the door, hoping Sean would catch up. Instead, Eddie fell into step. Parker shot me a look from the hallway. I pretended to be caught up in the crowd and disappeared around the corner. Eddie and I were on different paths now. I knew I was being mean to my old friend. It made me feel bad, like I was giving up part of myself.

When I got home that day, I pushed all the way to the back of my closet and hid the note in the pocket of a brown sport jacket I never wore. Then I took out my red reversible jersey. Mom had just washed it.

I rubbed the back of my hand against its soft sleeve. If I wore the red side out on Friday, who would find me on the front steps?

The night was silent except for the crunch of frostbitten grass under our feet. Kick and I dropped onto our backs on the golf-course putting green. The ground was cold, and my breath pulsed out of my mouth, disappearing. I pulled my jacket close.

"Look at them," Kick said. The stars were sprinkled across the sky as far as you could see. She scrunched over closer and squeezed my hand. "Makes me feel like a flyspeck."

"I like that feeling," I said, closing my eyes and lying still in the shivery-cold night.

In the swiftness of a moment, Kick rose up and I felt pressure on my lips. I opened my eyes, and she drew back. Then she reached down and kissed me again. Her mouth was soft and moist. It felt good. "Kiss me back," she whispered. I started to pump my lips. I was following the program! I shifted to be closer to her. But my move was too abrupt and my front teeth knocked into hers. "Ouch," she said, looking at me confused.

"Sorry." I glanced away. There was silence, and I heard Kick swallow.

"Guess we need practice," she said, rubbing her hand over mine. We started kissing again, just our lips at first, and then with our tongues. I rolled over on top of her, holding my weight above her. She put her arms around my back, and slowly slid one down to my butt.

"Touch my tattoo," she said. I put my fingers on her hip. "No, inside." She guided my hand under her pants. Her skin was warm and soft. I dove down on her lips again. We kissed for about twenty minutes, and then it got boring. I think Kick could have gone on all night.

I rolled off her and sat up.

"You know, you're a good kisser," she said.

"I am?"

"Mmhmm."

I licked my tongue over my front teeth and stared up at the stars. "Look, there's Orion." I showed Kick how to find him by his belt. "And there's Pegasus."

"How do you know them?"

"Uncle Mark and I used to lie out with a map of the stars. When I was younger."

"That sounds nice."

"It was."

"Can I ask you something? How come you never talk about your dad?"

I shrugged. "I hardly knew him. Only a few memories. Of him being sick, mostly." Kick took my hand. "But I have Uncle Mark. My mom's brother. He looks out for me."

"I want to meet him sometime."

"Okay." I felt the frost melting into my pants. "Kick, are you wet?"

"Yes," she said, jumping up. She pulled me from the ground. Walking to the car, I started to put my arm around her, hesitated, and pulled back. Would it say too much? It's what I was supposed to be doing. I reached over and plopped my arm on her shoulder. Kick slipped in against me. We must have been the image of young love, the two of us, entwined, making our way down the fairway under a canopy of stars.

If only things were how they looked.

I was edgy later that night. Tomorrow was the day I had been instructed to wear my red jersey.

We were up to the Byzantine Empire in world history: 800 AD. The controversy over icons. What did this have to do with *anything*? I bit at a hangnail, ripped it, and a drop of blood oozed out. Why was I nervous? I knew what to wear to school tomorrow. The jersey—gray side out.

When I woke the next morning, I tried to get back that feeling of being a flyspeck under the stars, but it wouldn't come. I pulled on my jersey. Never could wear the red side out again. Even though it had been my favorite. It seemed as if there should be a little funeral for it like the one I had when Cecil the frog died.

I was already seated in English class as Sean walked in. Was he looking at me? No. Yes, I think so. Did his head drop a little? Was he let down that I had on a gray shirt?

Parker seemed oblivious to me, let alone my clothes. If he was testing me, wouldn't he have been more pleased that I had passed? Eddie was so busy talking to Chloe Scanlon, the girl with all the rings in her ears, he didn't even look my way. The mystery would never be solved.

I couldn't pay attention in any of my classes. I kept wondering if someone was watching me. Someone gravely disappointed because I, David Olav Dahlgren, was wearing a gray shirt. Who was it? *It's not too late to find out,* said a voice inside. I jerked up. Of course it was. The clock said five minutes to three. The day was over. *Sneak out of study lab, run to the lavatory, and reverse your shirt,* the voice said. *You can be on the steps in your red jersey when the bell rings.*

My heart was pounding. Schmerdler, the lab supervisor, was on the other side of the room, working side by side with Jenny Melcher on her computer. I'd be out the door before she ever saw. *Go! Go!* the voice commanded. I carefully shut my book. Was I crazy? I slipped from my seat and sneaked out of the room. I raced to the bathroom, which was empty except for Sander Ogden taking a pee. I startled him and he jumped. Rumor had it he couldn't pee if anyone was nearby. The poor guy. He zipped up and skittered out the door. Someone more uncomfortable in his own skin than I was.

Adrenaline coursed through my veins. I ripped the jersey off, turned it inside out, and pulled it back on. I sprinted down the hallway and out the front door—driven by what, I did not know—to stand on the steps in my red jersey just as the shrill cry of the three o'clock bell sounded.

CHAPTER

THIRTEEN

The wind whipped at the tail of the jacket tied around my waist as I waited for the first students to trickle out of school. Another wave of dread passed over me. My armpits dripped like a soaker hose. Oh, *come on*. Whoever it was, just get out here.

I waited, watching out of the corner of my eye. Everyone who approached just went past me. What if whoever it was saw my gray shirt this morning and gave up? Was this how it would end? Like a firecracker that fizzled?

Then I saw Sean. He was with Parker and Rick Cutter. Parker was pointing at me. I started down the steps.

"Dahlgren," Parker called. "Where you going?" I sped up. "We need you for a game of b-ball!" he hollered.

I started running, afraid to look back, sure that they were roaring after me. I tore through the yards to my house, raced inside, and locked the door behind me. I ran to the back door, making sure it was tightly locked. Then I collapsed on the sofa.

All week I had been so sure of what to do and then, in just one moment . . . DAMN IT! I pressed my fist into my gut, imagining how fast this would spread around school, how they'd mock me.

The doorbell rang.

I didn't move. Ding-dong. Ding-dong. I slowly raised myself and peeked into the vestibule. I saw Sean standing at the door. He motioned to be let in.

"What do you want?" I called through the glass panes.

"In."

"Where's Parker and Cutter?"

"You can't play two-on-two with three guys."

I opened the door a crack. The screen door was still locked. He pointed at my red shirt. "You changed."

I peered out the side windows to see if Parker or anyone else was creeping around the house. "What do you care?"

Sean pulled back his hair and let it fall forward. "I sent you the note."

"What note? The one you wrote with Parker?"

"He doesn't know about it."

"Why did you come out of school with him?"

"I gave up on you."

"If you're lying . . ." I unlocked the screen door.

Sean pulled it open and slipped inside. He took in the living room with a glance; the frayed carpet and crack running the length of the wall. We looked at each other. I swallowed loudly. "Want to listen to some music?" I asked.

"Is anyone home?"

"No, my mom's still at work."

"Sure, let's hear some tunes."

"It's upstairs . . . in my room. I mean that's where my computer is. Upstairs." I pointed to the ceiling like an idiot.

He nodded. Smirking.

"Duck," I said as he went under the low overhang above the staircase. In my bedroom, I put on the Supremes.

Sean settled on my bed. "Why send the note?" I asked him. "Why not just say something?"

Sean grabbed my pillow and balled it up against his chest. "Wanted to be sure."

"You made me stand out there scared to death."

"Well, you did it." I looked at my guilty expression in the mirror. My heart pounded. He reached his arm out and started tickling me through my jeans. Shivers rushed up my belly into my chest. "Doesn't it feel amazing?" he asked.

He unbuttoned his pants. "Here," he said softly, grabbing my wrist and guiding me. My hand was shaking. Oh, God! My fingers closed. Solid.

Sean slipped his Calvin Klein's down, and I wriggled out of my jeans. I stared at his exquisite body and grabbed hold again. He reached for me. My hormones hit overdrive. I lost contact with Planet Earth.

I heard Sean making throaty noises, which grew more and more pronounced. He started pumping his hips, and I worked with the motion. His grunting got louder and louder. Suddenly, he let out a cry and popped. The sight of him made me go off too. Unbelievable!

Afterward, our eyes met and he looked away. I wanted to

pull a pillow over my head, to hide from the guilt that coursed through me. Sean jumped off the bed and pulled up his khakis. "I'm taking off," he said, bounding down the stairs.

"Wait!" I called, scrambling into my pants and following him. Where was he going so fast? I stepped out on the cold stoop in my sweat socks. "Want to eat dinner over?" No answer. He loped away down the block.

I rushed across the lawn, past the poplar tree creaking in the wind. "Let's do something!" I shouted from the middle of our neighbor's yard. Without answering, Sean disappeared behind the blue spruce that towered at the end of the street. I stared at the jagged branches, trying to catch one last glimpse, and then walked slowly back to my house.

"Hi, honey," Mom called, jiggling her keys out of the back door as I came in the front. She took me in with a glance. "How was your day?"

I dropped my gaze to the floor. I felt sticky. The smell of Sean was still on me. "Fine," I said, running upstairs to the bathroom to clean up. After fixing my bed, I came down again, grabbed my shoes and coat, and opened the back door.

"Where are you going?"

"Out."

"Be home by six," she called. "Grandma's coming for dinner."

I hopped on my bike and raced away, pushing down hard on the pedals—trying to drive away the sickening feeling that what we had done was wrong. I ended up at Lake Nokomis, where I used to swim as a kid. The lifeguards were long gone.

Even the row of buoys which marked the swimming area had been taken in. I ditched my bike and sat on the ground.

Sean! It had been him all along. I rolled my head back and forth, blades of grass brushing my neck, making plans in my head that I knew I should not be making. We could take a trip down to Stillwater, camp on the St. Croix. I'd wake up and find him outside the tent, cooking bacon and eggs over an open fire. If it got cold at night, we'd have to sleep in one bag. It wouldn't matter that I was gay. There *was* someone out there for me.

I sat up, shielding my eyes from the setting sun, and peered out over the lake. The rubber band still clung to my wrist. I grabbed it and began to pull, stretching it farther and farther. My eyes flinched shut. The band snapped, sharp against my skin, one last time, broke, and flew off into the lake. I felt sick.

"Hi, Mom," I said, sauntering into the kitchen after I returned home.

"Good, you're back. I'm going to pick up Grandma now." She checked a pot roast in the oven. "You set the table. And then clean your room. You have magazines lying all over in there."

"Sure, Mom," I said, heading upstairs with a garbage bag. *Hunting.* History. *Car and Driver.* Adios. *Guns & Ammo.* I took special pleasure in ripping that one in half. I stuffed them all in the trash bag, tied it tight, and lugged them out to the garage.

With my room clean, you could see the books again. I scanned the shelves and took out *Love in Another Town.* Back to violet-eyed beauties, jealous husbands, and aching vulnerability. *Thank God.*

CHAPTER

FOURTEEN

After dinner, I kept staring at my cell, willing it to ring. What was Sean doing right now? Babysitting his little sister? Didn't he want company? Or was he out with Parker? I imagined people gathering at Lake Calhoun, cruising around in cars, pulling up at the picnic tables near the lake where the in-crowd gathered. Would he rather be with them than me?

The phone rang. I jumped up and grabbed it. Kick.

"I am so bored," she said. "If I have to read one more page about the Middle goddamn Ages, I'll drop a toaster into my bath. Tell me something fun. Do you know any gossip?"

"Nobody tells me anything. You better call Eddie."

"I want to talk to you. Hey, you want to go to a party Saturday?"

"Okay. Whose party?"

"My cousin's turning twenty-one. She's having a band and everything."

"Will I know anyone?"

"Me. I'll take good care of you."

"Cool."

After Kick and I finished talking, the phone rang again. Maybe this time it was Sean. I picked up.

Eddie. "What's up?" I asked, annoyed.

"Can you do me a favor? It's an emergency."

"What?"

"I'm babysitting Willie, and we ran out of diapers. Could you get me a box of Pampers? We'll pay you back."

"Oh, come on. Can't you use something else?"

"What?"

"Paper towels and rubber bands?"

"You're going to be a terrible parent. Look—just go to the drugstore. It'll take ten minutes."

"Oh, all right."

When I got to Eddie's, Willie was running around the house naked, and Eddie was chasing him. They were both laughing. It made me want to have a little brother. Eddie got a diaper on him in short order and put the kid in bed with a bottle. I started to leave.

"Wait, I want to ask you something," Eddie said.

"What?"

He started gathering Willie's blocks into a big pile. "I'm wondering if you'll start a group with me at school."

"What kind of group?"

Eddie tossed a handful of blocks into a cardboard box. "The Gay/Straight Alliance."

I dropped into a swivel rocker. I feared this day would come, and now it had. "Why do you want to do that?"

He stopped picking up blocks and looked at me. "To find dates."

"Really?"

"No, we're going to get political. And give people a place to be themselves."

"Eddie"—I swiveled in the chair to face him—"you have no trouble being yourself. So why go superfag right now?"

"Why not?"

"Couldn't you wait until we graduate?"

"Nooo," he said. "I've waited long enough."

"What about your dad?"

"I don't think he'll be the parent adviser."

"He's gonna find out."

"You think he doesn't know? Have you seen the Jake Gyllenhaal posters in my bedroom? He's a jerk, but he's not stupid." Eddie set his jaw. "So, will you be at the first meeting or not?"

"Sorry. I'm not joining."

"But you're my friend. And, I thought, maybe . . . you weren't totally straight."

I stood up. "Well, I am."

"Great. You can be the 'alliance' part." He made those annoying quote marks again.

"Eddie, no straight guys are going to join." Just then we heard a crash, and Willie started howling. Eddie bolted up the stairs.

"I'm leaving, " I called up after him. I pulled open the front door and left. Eddie had finally come out. Now I was really going to have to steer clear of him at school.

That night, caught up in thoughts of Sean and what he would do next, I tossed and turned. I wanted to be with him badly. There were so many things I wanted to find out. Past midnight, I rose and went to my desk. I hadn't written poetry since seventh-grade English, but suddenly the desire to compose seized me. What rhymed with "Sean"? "Brawn"? "Lawn"? "Gone"?

After many drafts of really bad poems, I ripped up all my work except for two lines:

Now that we've jumped, taken the plunge,
I'll be the water and you be the sponge.

I opened the secret lining of my wallet and hid those words inside. Then I crawled under the covers, and clicked off the light.

Saturday afternoon I was taking a break from cleaning leaf glop out of the gutters when I heard my phone ring. I went inside and grabbed it. Sean!

"What are you doing?" he asked.

"Nothing." I saw that my hand was coating the phone with rotted leaves.

"Come over tonight."

"Okay. I mean, great."

"My parents are going out," Sean said.

"What time?"

"Seven."

"Should I eat first?"

"Nah, we'll order something."

"Who's coming?"

"It's not a party or anything. We'll just hang out, watch a movie."

"Uh-huh."

"See ya later," he said, hanging up.

Fantastic! It was already 4:00. I had to get the gutters done soon. I hoped I hadn't sounded too enthusiastic on the phone.

I grabbed my radio, took it up to the roof, and listened to oldies as I flung leaves. The ladder almost keeled over a few times, the way I was rocking to a Bob Dylan song.

Showering, I scrubbed everywhere and did my armpits twice. I tried on three different outfits before settling on black jeans and an aqua and black vintage bowling shirt with the name "Buzz" on the pocket. I slathered on cologne, gelled my hair, then washed it out.

Sean was waiting.

CHAPTER

FIFTEEN

As a rumble of thunder echoed in the distance, I rolled my bike out of the garage, avoiding the oil slick. Halfway there, a booming clap unleashed a downpour. My rain-slicked tires whisked down the sheeted asphalt. Splickety-lick. Splickety-lick. Splickety-lick. Rain slipped under my collar and ran down my back colder than ice cubes. The size of the houses grew bigger and bigger as I neared his neighborhood. I wondered what they did with all that inside space.

Drenched and shaking, I hurried up Sean's front steps and pounded on the door. He answered wearing sweatpants and a gray T-shirt. His breath smelled of beer. "You're soaked," he said, pulling me inside. I had a chill and couldn't stop shivering. "You want to go in the whirlpool?" he asked.

"You have one?" I pulled off my jacket and followed him up the stairs. Inside his parents' plush bedroom was a huge tiled bathroom with an oval tub double the usual size. Sean reached down, turned on the brass faucet. Hot water gushed out, steaming up the mirror. I peeled off the bowling shirt sticking to my skin.

Sean left and returned with two Old Milwaukee beers. "Chug it," he said, twisting the tops off the beer bottles and handing one to me. "Catch up." I tipped my head back, downed half in three gulps, breathed, and guzzled the rest. The steaming water in the tub inched closer to the top. Sean turned off the faucet and switched on the whirlpool jets. The bath swirled into motion.

"Get in," he said. I looked down, embarrassed to take off my pants.

He ducked out of the bathroom. "Getting more beer," he called over his shoulder.

I stripped off the rest of my wet clothing and draped it over a towel rack. My skin was red from the cold. I eased across the tiles and slipped into the circulating bubbles. Warmth flooded my body. Rushing water tickled my skin.

And then he appeared with two more bottles. In a flash, he exposed his body and disappeared under the bubbles. "Ahhh," he said. Our legs brushed under the water, and we stayed still for a minute.

"Feels so good," I said.

He laughed. For a few minutes we splashed around the tub, swigging our beers, and letting our skin touch under the bubbles. I could feel the beer going to my head. Suddenly, his hand was on me. Every nerve in my body tingled. I grabbed him back. Our breaths started coming faster and faster. He let out a little moan and rose up out of the water. I knew what he wanted and sat forward, opening my lips. . . . Sean let out a cry and flooded me. I swallowed. That surprised me.

I fell back into the water, choking a little and letting my face submerge into the bubbles. When I surfaced, Sean was stepping out of the tub.

He wouldn't look at me, but I glimpsed his tight expression in the mirror. I knew what was in his head. With all the excitement gone, guilt surged in. I took a swig of beer to rinse out the bittersweet taste in my mouth. I felt dirty.

Sean pulled open the bathroom door and went into his parents' room. The electronic trill of my phone sounded. Someone knew! I ignored the ringing, thankful whoever it was didn't leave a message.

"When you're dry," Sean called over his shoulder, "I'll be downstairs." I leaned back as the water whirled around me.

Climbing out of the tub, I thought we should never do this again, and wondered how to make it last longer next time. My clothes were still wet, so I wrapped up in an oversize towel and went downstairs, embarrassed by my nakedness, by what we'd done.

"Wonton soup, large," Sean said into the phone as he read from the paper menu. "Shrimp fried rice, large. Mu shu pork, large. Egg rolls and extra duck sauce." He hung up and looked at me. "I'm starving."

"Me too." I stood next to him, letting my arm brush against his. He pulled away. "Could I borrow some clothes?"

Sean went upstairs and got one of his sweaters and some old jeans. As I pulled the soft navy-blue V-neck over my head, I smelled his scent.

I tried to watch TV in the family room while Sean drove to

get the food. But all I could think about was that we had done something really bad.

Sean was back in fifteen minutes, pulling the steaming containers out of the white bag and putting them on the coffee table. "Dive in," he said as he grabbed the fried rice and dropped himself onto the couch in front of the TV. I took a mu shu pancake, spread it with duck sauce, and heaped on shredded pork. I wolfed down the oozing creation and made another. Our shoulders touched, and I blurted out the question I had been wanting to ask. "How long have you known?"

"What?"

"That you're . . . you know, that you like guys."

"I don't. I like getting off." Sean set down his carton of fried rice. "I want to get married and have kids."

I was beginning to doubt that it would work out that way for me. Sean picked up the remote and started flipping channels. "Guys fool around, you know. Nobody talks about it, that's all."

"Who else have you fooled around with?"

He made a face at me. "I don't kiss or write love poems."

"Right," I said, stomach sinking.

"And besides," he said, "I don't put it in my mouth."

My ears turned hot and red.

We watched reruns for a while, and then Sean grabbed my arm. "Hey! You rinsed out the tub, didn't you?" I shook my head. We raced upstairs and cleaned his parents' bathroom, using Windex and everything.

Afterward, Sean sat on the staircase near the front door.

"You want me to go?" I asked.

"I'm kind of tired."

"It's only nine o'clock."

Sean shrugged. "All right," I said. I shook my head and looked down at the floor.

"Well, I suppose we could play some Ping-Pong," he offered.

"Really?" I brightened.

We went downstairs and played five games. Sean lost himself in trying to beat me. For a little while it felt like we were just friends. And then, remembering why we weren't, my heart sank.

After the Ping-Pong I said I should be going. But my clothes weren't dry yet. Sean stuffed them into a plastic grocery bag and let me wear his stuff home.

As I pulled open the front door, he grabbed my shoulders from behind and whispered in my ear. "Don't ever tell anyone about tonight."

"Okay."

"Promise?"

"Yes."

"Swear to God?"

"Yessss." The wooden door closed behind me.

I glided toward home through the misty streets, dodging the water still dripping from the trees. Was it raining again? Or not? The sky couldn't seem to make up its mind. I wondered if straight guys really experimented as much as Sean thought. Or said, at least. Maybe. Though I don't think they enjoyed it like I did or like Sean seemed to, however much he wanted to believe that.

CHAPTER

SIXTEEN

Mom scraped another crusty helping of hash browns out of the black skillet and heaped them onto my yolk-swirled plate. My phone rang and I answered.

"Did you forget?" Kick's indignant voice asked.

"Forget what?"

"David! The party last night."

"Ohhh!" I let out a breath. I had said I would go with her.

"Where were you?" she asked.

"Ummm . . ."

"Your mom said you were at Sean's, but you didn't answer your cell."

"I forgot to charge it." I wrinkled my nose at the lie. There was a long silence, and then Kick said quietly: "You didn't want to be with me."

"Yes, I did. It's just that . . . I forgot." I realized how bad that sounded. I was making her feel worse. "I'm sorry. Can I make it up to you?"

"How?"

"Take you to the movies and buy you a giant bag of malted milk balls."

"You're cruel. You know I can't eat them."

"Fat-free cookies then?"

"Any movie I want?"

"Hopefully a chick flick."

"Fine. But you're still on probation, absentminded one."

"Kick, you're the best." She really was.

Later, sitting in the back of the theater, our legs slung over the chairs in front of us, we kissed a few times, but I really wanted to see the movie. Kick sighed, and rested her head on my shoulder. I softly stroked her hair. Maybe this could still happen.

By English on Monday, it seemed like a month since I had last seen Sean. I glanced at him as he slipped behind his desk, but he didn't look my way. All through the lecture, I kept wanting to turn around.

After class, I fell in with him and Parker in the hallway. Then Jenny Melcher and a friend of hers named Brenda came around the corner. Parker and Sean started talking to them. Standing there silent, as Sean flirted with Brenda, I wondered if he even noticed I was there.

That had me stewing all day. After the final bell rang, I had to go to Sean's locker. "Sean!" I sort of yelled, speeding up my pace when I saw him leaving.

"Be cool," he growled under his breath as I came up to him.

"Sorry."

Sean started down the hallway, and I went with him. "Want to do something?" I asked.

He looked annoyed. "Not today."

I kept walking with him to the front door, but he went out without me.

I hadn't gotten the fix I needed. Now he was gone. So I needed it even more. Hormones were ruining my life.

CHAPTER

SEVENTEEN

By the weekend, I couldn't eat, couldn't sleep, couldn't think of anything but him. I was convinced that he had lost all interest, that we were done, that I would be alone my whole life. Then he called.

"You going to Parker's Halloween party tonight?" he asked.

"Yeah," I said.

"Who with?"

"Kick."

"I'm going with Brenda. Come over here first, okay? The house is all mine this weekend."

"Great."

After Sean hung up, I fell onto the bed and wiggled my legs in the air like a terrier getting his belly scratched.

I didn't know what Brenda was supposed to be when she opened the door to let us into Sean's house. She wore this short silky dress, platinum-blond wig, push-up bra, and high-heel sandals. "You a hooker?" I asked. Sean laughed.

"Ever heard of Marilyn Monroe?" she replied sharply, plumping her wig.

Sean was dressed as an accident victim, his head wrapped in gauze.

He came over and grabbed my shoulder. "Nice World War Two regalia." I puffed up my chest so the medals showed.

"I went to Grandma's closet for mine," Kick announced, showing off her 1920s flapper dress. "Mmm, dahling," she said, touching me, "uniforms are so sexy."

Sean made rum and Cokes for us, refilling his father's Bacardi bottle with water, then leading us into the living room. Sean and Brenda settled on the overstuffed sofa, Kick and me on the love seat.

"Let's take pictures," Brenda said, jumping up. Which turned out to be about a hundred shots of her and Sean. "Does it have a timer?" Kick asked. "Take one with all of us." Sean set the camera up pointed toward Brenda, Kick, and me on the sofa. Then he ran back and dove across our legs. I swear, just after the camera flashed, he pressed his hand down into my lap.

Parker's street was jammed with cars. Even from where we had to park, you could hear the party bubbling up inside his house. He and Jenny Melcher met us at the door, dressed punk—complete with black leather jackets, safety-pin earrings, and matching red streaks in their hair. "About time you got here," Parker said as he slapped Sean on the shoulder.

Kick and I followed Sean and Brenda through the crowd of vampires, ghouls, and angels and went down the stairs.

Brenda pulled Sean into a small circle. I turned and looked at Kick. "See anyone you want to talk to?"

"Just you," she said, tracing the outline of the lieutenant's stripes on my shoulder. I eyed Sean on the couch. Brenda was on his lap now, and they were laughing.

"Come on." I tugged on Kick's arm. "Let's see what there is to eat."

Upstairs in the candlelit dining room, gruesome creations crowded the table. A gelatinous, pinkish-gray brain stood in the center. Jell-O. Little ear-shaped pasta lay covered in bloodred sauce. Black potato chips, mini-franks bobbing in ketchup, and peeled-grape eyeballs stood ready for the taking. Amputated mannequin hands, palm sides up, spilled candy corn. At the far end of the table was a platter of something that looked like dog poo.

As I pondered the table, someone came up from behind and covered my eyes. "Guess who." The raspy voice was alarmingly familiar, but I couldn't place it. "Guess—or I'll sprinkle fairy dust on you." I spun around and opened my eyes to face Parker's mother decked out as the good witch Glinda. "David," she said grabbing my arm, "how *are* you?" She twirled to display her elaborate costume and then stood there smiling. Was I supposed to tell her how great she looked? I desperately tried to signal Kick, who was happily eating grape eyeballs.

"The food's really . . . gross," I blurted out.

"Isn't it?" She reached for my hand. "Come see what other horrible goodies I made."

I let my hand rest in hers a moment. Could anyone see us?

"Come along now," she said, brushing my cheek. "You can be my taster."

Why me? I started to freak. With one deliberate motion, I slid sideways to the table, put my arm around Kick, and yanked her to my side. "Have you two met?" Kick knew how to talk to mothers. I'd always liked that about her. Once extracted from the clutches of Glinda, we headed for the party downstairs. Icy buckets of beer and pop sat on the floor. I helped myself to a beer, and Kick took a diet soda.

An oversize leather chair in the corner beckoned, and we squeezed into it, Kick on my lap, watching the crowd. She fed me bites of the chocolate dog-poo brownie. Other couples were kissing, and I think that's what she wanted. But not in front of all these people.

I stood, lifting her off me. Jostling people, we pushed through the partying throng. In the crush, Kick's hand grabbed my ass. Yikes! Sean knocked back a beer as Brenda held with both hands the arm he draped over her.

I led Kick to the sliding glass doors facing the patio, pulled them open, and stepped through, glad to be clear of the over-heated party. "More private," I said.

"Mmhmm." Kick snuggled next to me, and I put my arm around her. With closed eyes and open lips, she turned toward me. I pressed my lips to hers. We kissed, standing near the gas grill, ignoring the wintry wind. I longed for my jacket and shuddered.

"Oh, God! I know," Kick said. She pushed her body hard

against me and lifted my hand to her breast as she continued devouring my lips.

I squeezed and kissed her back. But I was freezing. How come Kick didn't notice? Finally, I broke our embrace and began jumping up and down. "It's cold."

"Poor baby," she said.

I hurried us back inside, relieved we were done kissing for now, and excused myself to go to the bathroom. While I peed, a tap on the door startled me. Just when I was really hating myself, Sean slipped inside.

"What are you doing?" I craned my neck to look at him.

"Shhhh." He closed the door and joined me at the toilet bowl. He let loose a stream as I zipped up.

"Want to dump these girls?" he asked.

"What do you mean?"

"Have some fun?"

"How?"

He finished and grinned broadly. "Figure it out. And then come over." Sean lost his balance and took a step back to recover. Then he left.

The party dragged on. I kept hoping Sean and Brenda would leave so we could too, but he was growing more and more animated. Kick and I went into the poolroom and played eight ball with Mona and her boyfriend.

I managed to pocket the cue ball, losing the game for us, and just as I did, Parker called to me from upstairs. I went up and found him standing, propping Sean up with his shoulder. "Will you take him home?" Parker asked. "He's tanked."

Parker dug in Sean's pockets. Sean smiled and swatted at his hands. "Whatcha doin'?" Parker pulled out the car keys. "Hey, those are my keesh."

"David's borrowing them," Parker explained as he tossed them to me.

"Buddy," Sean said, throwing his arm around me, grinning stupidly. Parker and I led him outside and laid him down in the backseat. Kick and Brenda came out, and we started off. We hadn't gone ten blocks when Sean rose up from where he lay in Brenda's lap. "Stop!" he cried, opening the back door while the car was moving. I slammed on the brakes, and Sean dove out. Silently, facing forward, we all listened to him retch.

"Real nice," Brenda said as he struggled back into the car.

Kick handed Sean a bottle of water from her leather bag. "Rinse your mouth," she told him.

He took a gulp and then fell back on the seat. When I dropped Brenda off at her house, there were no romantic good-byes between her and Sean. He was dead to the world.

I turned the car toward Kick's. When we parked in front of her house, she ran her fingernails along my thigh. She obviously wanted to continue where we'd left off at the party. "With Sean right there?" I whispered.

Kick laughed. "You think he'd be traumatized? Anyway, he's passed out."

Okay, if that's what she wanted. I took a deep breath and

started kissing her, imagining that I was in the backseat with Sean.

As Kick's hand rubbed up and down my thigh and I kissed her neck, Sean suddenly lurched up. He stared at us. "Whuh?"

Kick laughed. "Go back to sleep, baby."

"Nooo," he wailed. "Take me home. I feel like shit."

"I better take him."

"Okay," Kick replied. "Then come back."

"He might need someone."

"He's just drunk."

"Well . . . Okay, if I can." We walked to the door and I gave her a kiss. We both knew I wasn't coming back that night.

Sean was asleep when we reached his house, but I managed to rouse him and take him inside. He clung to me, and I didn't care that he smelled of puke. But I made him go to the bathroom to wash his face and brush his teeth. He followed my directions (though I hadn't told him to sit on the floor while brushing). Helping him out of his jeans and sweater was an exercise in self-restraint. But the moment was almost here. Depositing him under the covers, I put out the light. Every inch of my skin tingled as I slid in next to him. Inside I was terrified.

I moved over in Sean's bed until my shoulder was ever so slightly pressed against his and waited. "Sean," I whispered. No response. "Sean." I grabbed his arm and jiggled it. Just rhythmic breathing. "SEAN!"

I clicked on the lamp next to the bed. He didn't move. I shook him. Nothing. Then I lifted one of his eyelids. A zombie.

Slapping the mattress near his head, I yelled, "Sean! Get up!" It was useless.

I threw back the covers and went downstairs. Cheesecake in the refrigerator called to me. Creamy and delicious. I phoned my mother and told her I was staying at Sean's for the night. I wasn't going to leave him. You can choke to death on your own vomit when you're that drunk.

Back upstairs, Sean was still out cold. I wandered around his room, looking at his closet stuffed with clothes, his books, the array of colognes on his dresser. Carefully opening his wallet, I discovered a fake ID that said he was twenty-one. Where did he go with that?

CREAK! The huge old house groaned. I jumped a foot and slapped Sean's wallet down. Waiting a moment to catch my breath, I opened the top drawer of his dresser. The built-in compartments were full of stuff: first-place ribbons, a letter from his eighth-grade teacher saying what promise he had, a package of gummy worms, wallet pictures of him and Brenda, an iPod nano, and a star sapphire ring, which I tried on. The rest of the drawers were filled with clothes, which I poked through quickly. At the very bottom of one drawer I noticed a paper bag. I opened it to find old *People* magazines. What was he saving those for? I rifled through them. Then I saw it. On the bottom of the bag. *Playgirl*. Two of them. Sean had *Playgirl*! I grabbed one and flipped open the pages, then took it back to bed with me and paged through it excitedly.

Carefully replacing the magazines and snapping off the light again, I nudged Sean. "You still asleep?" Gingerly, I put my arms around him. He didn't stir. I pulled him to me. His skin was warm and soft. I tucked my head under his chin and hugged. If he were awake, would he squeeze back? Would I even be here?

I reached down and felt for him, hoping that he would respond, but he didn't. It felt good to cop a feel. I rolled away, fantasizing what might have happened, and found relief.

As I started to drift off, I put my arm on his chest, noticing his heartbeat. Thump, thump, thump. I pressed my palm flat against his breast to better sense it. Thump, thump. There was something soothing about it. Right here within reach of my hand. It was hypnotic. I gathered the covers snugly around us, dropped my head onto the pillow, and fell asleep; one hand sensing Sean's heartbeat, the other, my own.

About five a.m., I heard Sean stumble out of bed. Hoping he didn't mind my being there, I got up and followed him into the can. "My head," he said, fighting to get the childproof cap off the aspirin. I helped him shake out three pills, and he gulped them down. He looked at me sheepishly. "Did I puke last night?"

"In the street. We all heard you."

Sean groaned as he groped his way along the wall back to bed. Getting under the covers in the fetal position, he pressed the pillow over his head. I slipped in next to him, reaching for his shoulders and gently rubbing them. He didn't respond, so I dropped my hand. That brought whimpers, so I started up again. Ever so slowly, while rubbing his back, I moved toward him, poised to cup my body around his. He felt my presence, pushed back, and we fell asleep like that.

CHAPTER

EIGHTEEN

I was shoveling in the last bite of chunk turkey over mashed potatoes when Parker sat down next to me at the lunchroom table. "Come on. You've got to see this."

Striding just a step ahead of me, Parker led the way to Coach's office where he pulled out the Whitman Academy record book and pointed to his freshly added name. Why didn't Sean join us? I looked for him down every hallway these days.

The bell rang, and Parker and I started for fourth-period math when I saw the bright yellow poster with the unmistakable heading. Dear God, don't let Parker notice.

"Fuck, what is that?" he exclaimed, stopping to read it:

Gay/Straight Alliance
Organizing Meeting
November 11
3:30 p.m.
Room 321
All students and faculty welcome!

Parker checked over his shoulder and then pulled a pen out of his pocket. He started drawing on the poster.

"Don't," I said.

"Why not?" He laughed, and with a few quick loops, drew a dick and balls over the carefully hand-lettered poster. "I don't get fags," he said as we hurried away. "Do you?"

All through math I kept glancing at Parker's unperturbed face. Didn't he have the slightest bit of awareness? I made up my mind to say something when we got out in the hallway, to tell Parker off. The bell rang, and we spilled out of class. But I couldn't do it. When I got to my locker, I fired my books inside and kicked the door closed. Why did Eddie have to stick that screaming-yellow poster in everyone's face! Who in the hell was going to that meeting? Eddie and some girls. That was it.

Sean and I played one-on-one basketball in his driveway after school. "Sean, I told you to give me whatever needs to go in the laundry," his mother called, leaning out the door.

"Mom, we've got a game going. Just take whatever needs it."

"How do I know?" she asked. "It's all on the floor."

"If it's on the floor, it needs it."

She went back in the house, shaking her head. Twenty minutes later we were standing in front of Sean's open refrigerator, taking turns drinking orange juice from the carton. Sean's mother walked into the kitchen and leveled her gaze at him. Her eyes were fierce. Sean swung the fridge door shut. "What?"

She just stood there staring. "David had better go," she said emphatically, without glancing in my direction.

"Why?"

"Sean? Did you hear me?"

"Whoa, look at the time," I said. It must be bad if she had to send me home before she started yelling at him. "Getting late," I mumbled. Sean followed as I darted for the front door. "What's going on?" I whispered.

"She's pissed about something."

"Call me."

As Sean disappeared behind the door, I shivered to think of him returning to face his mother. That was one scary look.

CHAPTER

NINETEEN

I waited all evening for Sean to call, but my phone was ominously silent. In second period the next day, when Detweiler started his lecture, Sean's desk was empty. Was he sick? He seemed fine the day before. I got a bad feeling.

Instead of going to math, I went outside and dialed Sean's number, praying that he would answer. But he didn't.

That evening, I couldn't stand it any longer. If Sean didn't answer, I was heading over there. Calling as soon as the dishes were done, I got him.

"I can't talk," he said, and hung up.

I flopped on my bed facedown. At midnight, I gave up hope that he would call back. I undressed, punched my pillow into shape, and finally fell asleep.

When Sean didn't show up in English again the next morning, I worked myself into a state. Calling again and again, voicemail always picked up. I texted him, but he didn't reply. What had happened?

And then Friday morning, there he was, sexy as hell,

slipping his long legs under the desk in Detweiler's class. Our eyes met, and it was as if he hadn't seen me.

I staked out his locker after school until he showed up. "What's wrong?" I asked as he dialed the combination on his lock. "How come you weren't in school?"

He shrugged.

"Were you sick?"

"Not really," he said, grabbing his jacket and closing the locker. "I gotta go."

"Couldn't we talk for a minute?"

"Kind of in a hurry," he said, walking away.

"Will you call me?" I asked. But he pretended not to hear.

Riding by Jolly's Art Supply on Sunday, I decided to splurge on stationery. It was time to send another letter to Barbara Taylor Bradford. I locked my bike to a No Parking sign and went inside. The sun's long rays fell on the hardwood floor. A smell of rubber cement filled the air.

Walking down one of the aisles, I stopped short. Eddie! I backtracked out of view. He was standing on a step stool, pulling sheets of yellow poster board off a high shelf. Turning and starting for the door, I got caught.

"Hey, David," he called from his perch. Carrying the poster board, he got down from the stool and walked over. "It's the boy wonder," he said snidely.

"What are you talking about?"

That evoked laughter. "I'm going to Chloe's," he said. "We're making posters. Want to come?"

"I can't."

Eddie shrugged and placed his poster board on the check-out counter. "Kick's been giving me an earful about you."

I ignored his comment. Eddie would have blithely launched into any subject in public, no matter how embarrassing. He paid and headed for the door. Skipping the stationery, I followed him.

"So, what did Kick say about me?" I asked.

"She wants you, baby." Eddie put his fingers up to his lips in a vee and flicked his tongue through them.

The blood rushed to my ears. "Don't be a jerk, okay?"

"Who, me?"

"Yeah."

"Why can't you get it up for her?" Eddie asked loudly, so anyone on the street could hear. "That's what I want to know."

"Same reason I can't get it up for you, dickhead."

Eddie laughed. "I like your bitchiness."

That made me chuckle, despite myself. Eddie knew me well. Why was I so mean to him?

The cold stung my bare legs as I jogged to Lake Calhoun very early Monday morning. A mist rose off the water. Finding a bench in the dull morning light, I sat down to wait in the stillness. No one was out yet.

Word hadn't come from Sean the whole weekend. I had to see him. He ran here in the mornings.

After twenty minutes, my nose started to run and my legs turned red. But I didn't care if I got frostbite. I kept waiting. Then, off in the distance, I saw him jogging in my direction.

I turned away so he wouldn't recognize me. The step-pad, step-pad of his footfalls lulled me as he approached. This was my opportunity. "Wait! Sean!" I called, jumping up.

"What are you doing here?" he asked without stopping.

I started running. "Waiting for you." No response. "What's going on? Why was your mom so mad that day?"

He shook his head. "None of your business."

"Tell me."

"Okay. She found some *Playboys*."

"*Playboys*!" I sped up to keep pace with him. "You mean *Playgirls?*"

"How do you know?"

"I . . . I saw them in your dresser."

"You saw them?"

"Okay, I was snooping," I said between breaths. "What happened?"

"I said they were yours."

"What!" I careened to a halt, grabbing Sean's arm and jerking him to a stop.

"You told your mom they were mine?"

"Yeah. That your mom goes through your things so you asked me to keep them."

"My mother doesn't go through my things."

"Serves you right for jerking off with 'em while I was passed out."

I shook my head. "Thanks a lot."

"You think she believed me? Took me to a shrink."

"Really?"

He looked over at me. "I had to promise her. . . ."

"What?"

"That I wouldn't hang out with you anymore." Sean stared at the ground.

My body trembled. "What does that mean? We're going to have to sneak around?" Sean shook his head. "What then?"

"Sorry, David." He put a hand on my shoulder. "I really am." He started walking.

I followed. "Why are you listening to her?" Sean wouldn't look at me. He broke into a run. I matched him step for step. "C'mon," I pleaded. "We can still be friends."

Sean sped up till we were sprinting, our breaths coming faster and faster. "Stop!" I shouted. He kept running, so I clamped onto his arm. He wrenched free of my grip. What was the use? Sean looked back once to make sure I wasn't following as he put more and more distance between us until he disappeared.

CHAPTER

TWENTY

I lay in the grass along Lake Calhoun, staring into the cloudless sky, dimly conscious that classes had already started. The tubalike honking of a distant car horn roused me. Lifting my head, I glanced in the direction of Whitman. Would anyone notice that I was gone?

Schmerdler would, of course. During homeroom, she would gleefully record this fact in her computer. If she called my mother to see where I was, they'd find out I was skipping school. They wouldn't know yet that I was never going back.

I thought I heard birds chirruping in the distance, but it turned out to be a class of preschoolers walking hand in hand. Their high voices sounded so cheerful. Those were the days. You had your buddy, and you didn't let go.

I got up and walked down to the water. Long past swimming season, the docks were all taken in. The lake would freeze soon.

The world was awake and bustling now. Two women launched a canoe. A pair of runners in bright fleece jackets jogged by. Meandering along the path, a mother pushed twins in a double stroller, soaking up the low rays of morning sun. Everyone but me seemed to have someone.

I looked at my watch: 9:35. English class had started, and Sean would be sitting at a desk behind mine. Only I wouldn't be there. Would he notice?

A blast of wind hit me in the back, and I pulled my sweatshirt jacket tight over my hunched shoulders. I walked away from the lake to the rows of old houses lining the streets near Lakewood Cemetery. Escaping barefoot out the front door of his tall wooden house, a toddler squealed in delight. His mother was right behind. She grabbed the child, whirled him in the air, and ran with him back inside, laughing. What would it feel like to be a father? With little kiddies jumping up and down at the door when you came home from work?

Lingering there too long, I feared that someone might think I was up to something. I turned and skulked up the street, wondering whether science would ever develop gene therapy to make me straight.

I came upon the cemetery, rolling hills overlooking the lake, studded with limestone monuments. All those dead people had a really nice view. I made my way to the wrought-iron fence by the edge of Lake Calhoun, reading the markers as I went, careful not to step on the graves and make bad luck.

One marker said "Michael Elmstead, Beloved Son." He died at the age of twenty-two. I shivered.

As I stood there in the wind, an itch in my throat made me

cough. I cleared my throat, but the itch was still there. I tried again and again, but couldn't get rid of the scratchy feeling. I put my hand to my forehead. Hot. Suddenly, I didn't feel so good.

Mom found me in bed when she got home from work. She came back a few minutes later with tea, and rye toast with butter. I sat up and sipped the tea. The hot minty water soothed my throat. Mom sat and watched me eat, asking how I felt. I was glad she was home taking care of me, but I didn't want her hanging out in my room. After I handed her the dirty plate and lay back down with the pillow over my head, she left.

When she closed my door, I climbed out of bed and found the navy-blue sweater Sean had given me on the night of the rainstorm. Burying my face in it, smelling him, I started crying. He had made up his mind. It was over.

TWENTY-ONE

The next two days passed without a trace. I stayed home and eventually my fever passed. No one felt sorry for me. Which wasn't fair. When someone you loved broke up with you, that's when friends were supposed to take you out for dessert and let you talk nonstop about your breakup.

But no one knew Sean and I had broken up. They didn't even know we were together. Well, we weren't together. I was together. He was just horny.

Left alone with my despairing thoughts, I almost wished Eddie would call. But he didn't.

I checked the secret compartment of my wallet and found the poem I had written. Hurling myself onto the bed, I covered my face.

"David, you're going to be late." The next morning Mom was shaking me awake.

"Still don't feel good," I said, moaning.

"Then you should see a doctor."

"Uh-uh."

Mom began picking up the clothes strewn all over the floor. "One or the other," she said. "School or the doctor."

"I'm not going back to school." I thought I'd send up a trial balloon.

"What?" She leveled her gaze at me. "Yes, you are."

"I'm getting a job."

"David," she said, sitting on the bed, "what's happened?"

"Nothing."

"Are you in trouble?"

"No." I looked away.

"You can tell me."

"I'm not."

"What's this about then?"

I saw it was hopeless. "I'm just tired of school."

"That's no excuse. You're going to college."

"Mom, aren't you late for work?"

Slowly, she stood, studying my face. "This is your last sick day. Tomorrow, you go back."

An advertisement I had seen on a bus stop came to mind. For a gay hotline. I guess you were supposed to call before you committed suicide. What would it be like to talk to someone there? Out of curiosity, I wanted to see if the listing came up on Google. I typed in "gay hotline," and there it was for anyone brave enough to call.

I went to school the next day, wanting to race up to English as soon as first period was over, but holding back, afraid to find out how Sean would react to me. At the last minute, I slipped into my seat.

When the bell rang, the class emptied into the hall. I caught Sean's eye. He nodded, just barely, and looked away. Then Brenda showed up, feeding him pieces of muffin like it was wedding cake or something. I thought I was going to puke.

CHAPTER

TWENTY-TWO

Did you ever want to be a woodchuck pawing away the cold, crumbling earth, burying yourself for a long, long sleep? Disappearing so no one could see you or touch you or hurt you? Lying on the patchy grass under the hickory tree in the backyard, I clawed at the soil with my fingernails. My cheeks burned in the biting November cold.

"David!" Mom called as the storm door on the back stoop slapped open in the wind. "You were just sick." I watched her start down the steps and thought about jumping up on my haunches and scampering away. Like we were in a Kafka story. But her face looked worried. "I'm okay," I said, getting up on my two legs. She looped her arm around me.

"Mom!" I protested, shrugging her off.

We went inside and watched a rerun of *Will & Grace*. Did she secretly have a crush on Will? Well, so did I. Which was weird. Having the same crush as my mother. But at least she liked the show.

Later, she drove over to look in on Grandma, who had been

feeling weak. Sitting at the kitchen table, I tried to do math. I kept messing up and erasing my answer until the paper ripped.

I flung the pencil across the room, pushed up out of the chair, and started pacing around the kitchen. There was no one to talk to. Or was there? I went upstairs and Googled "gay hotline" again, 888–843–4564. Just hit those numbers, and someone gay would pick up. I opened the phone, held my breath, and dialed.

A man answered. "Gay and Lesbian Hotline. Jim speaking." I didn't say anything. "Hello? Is someone there?" he asked.

"Hi," I said, swallowing, so it came out more like a croak.

"Oh, there you are. How you doing tonight?"

My breath was coming hard. I drilled my finger down on the disconnect button.

What was I supposed to say to a complete stranger?

After school the next day, I dialed the hotline number again. What a jerk I had been to hang up the night before. "Be cool," I whispered to myself as the line rang.

"Gay and Lesbian Hotline," a voice answered. A *woman's* voice. I slammed the phone shut. Shit! I did it again.

Almost a week went by before I got up the nerve to call again. I kept my eyes closed while the phone was ringing.

And then he answered. Jim. From last Wednesday. "It's you," I said.

"Yes, it's me," he replied. "Who's this?"

"Um, you don't know me. I called last week and hung up."

"Well, don't be afraid of me. Unless you see me in a swimsuit. Now that's frightening." I laughed a little bit. "Anything you wanted to talk about?" he asked. "Not that we have to have anything special to talk about. I mean we can just chat."

"Okay."

"Mind if I ask how old you are?"

"Sixteen."

"Oh." He sighed. "I remember being sixteen. Hard year."

I started nodding as if he could see me.

"So tell me what's going on. Are you in school?"

"Uh-huh."

"And you think you might be gay?"

"Uh-huh."

"Do you have anyone to talk to?"

"No." I tried to fight it back, but the tears came. I'm sure he could hear.

"Is there someone you could tell? A friend?"

"I can't tell Eddie," I said.

"Why not?"

"Then half the school would know."

"Is there someone you trust?"

"My friend Kick. Only, she's sort of my girlfriend."

"Oh, dear. Well, you're in good company. The first person I came out to was my high-school girlfriend."

"Really? What happened?"

"She was surprised at first. And then she cried. We broke up that night. But in the end, I think she was relieved."

"Why?"

"She thought there was something wrong with her. Because I was so uninterested."

"Oh."

"She knew then it was me, not her."

"Are you still friends?"

"We're in touch."

"But you're not friends."

"That was a long time ago. We stayed friendly through high school and college. Then she got married and moved to San Diego."

There was a pause. I wanted to keep talking, but I couldn't think of what to say.

"Are there gay teachers at your school?" Jim asked.

"I don't know." I thought of Mr. Detweiler.

The headlights of my mother's car flashed as she turned into the driveway. "Jim! I have to go."

"Why? Don't hang up."

"My mom's home."

"Call me again. I'm here from seven to eleven, Wednesday nights."

"Okay."

"What's your name?"

"Umm, Bob," I said.

"Take care, Bob."

I hung up, raced to my room, and dove onto the bed. I could have talked to Jim all night. Now, it would be seven days until I could call him again.

CHAPTER

TWENTY-THREE

Saturday night Kick and I went to the movies. Sitting in our own row on the side, I put my arm around her. After a little while, I could feel Kick looking at me instead of the movie. I pulled her close and planted a quick one on her lips. "Let's watch," I whispered, and sunk back into my seat. All my attention was on the hunky male lead.

Afterward, we went out cruising in Kick's car.

"Let's go," Kick said as we passed Minnehaha Falls. "See the falls."

We parked in the empty lot and walked down to the overlook. The rushing white water, falling from its high stone ledge, crashed into the black pool below. "Isn't it beautiful?" Kick inched next to me, her arms around my waist.

"I like the way it sounds," I said. She looked up at me, and I kissed her as she pressed her body into mine. We started making out, and it felt wrong. Why was I doing this? I stopped kissing her.

"What's the matter?" she asked. "Don't you like to kiss?" I stood there, not knowing what to say. Kick broke away from me and walked back to the car. Should I tell her? She turned the radio up as we cruised along the parkway.

Pulling up in front of my house, I grabbed her hand. I had to do this. "Kick."

"What?" she asked, her face dimly lit by the streetlight.

"I have to tell you something."

"What?"

"You can never tell anyone."

Kick turned off the music. "I won't."

"Including Eddie. *Especially* Eddie."

"Yes, yes."

"I think, well . . ."

"What is it?"

"This is hard."

"Come on."

"Well, I think I'm . . . gay."

Kick flinched. "You?" I nodded. "What makes you think so?"

"The way I feel."

"What do you mean?"

"The way I feel about someone."

"A guy?"

"Yeah."

"Who?"

"I can't say."

"David! Someone at school?"

"Well . . ."

"It is!" Kick fingered the silver turtle on her charm bracelet. "David, I *have* to know."

"He'd kill me if I told you."

"*Pleeeaase.*"

"Sean."

"*He's* gay?"

"Sometimes."

"Oh my God. I feel so dumb." Kick stared at her lap, blinking back tears. "So, what about me?"

"Maybe we can be like Will and Grace," I stupidly said. She turned the key in the ignition, and the car jumped to a start.

"Do you hate me?" I asked.

"Oh, David, no. I'm just shocked." We sat there, not talking, listening to the Volvo idle.

"Kick, I'm so sorry."

"You don't have to say that."

"But I am." I got out of the car and bent down to see her, lingering, with the door open, hoping she would say something else. She tried to smile, only it made her look sad. "I'll call you," I said softly, closing the door. She hit the accelerator. I listened to the belly of her car scraping asphalt as she sped off along the potholed street.

CHAPTER

TWENTY-FOUR

Mom made me go to church on Sunday and we got there late. We had to sit in the front pew, right under a nearly naked plaster statue of Jesus on the cross. When the Lord's Prayer came, I looked up, inspecting the folds of the loincloth, trying to imagine what was underneath. This is what I had sunk to. Checking out Jesus.

Mom put a venison roast in the oven for Sunday dinner. The meat of a deer that my cousin shot. No way was I eating it.

With Mom busy in the kitchen, I sat on the front steps under the gray sky. The cold of the cement soaked through my jeans. How was Kick doing? Crying? Cutting my face out of all the pictures of us? Not that I was a great catch, but she seemed to think so. I loved that about her.

Should I call her? Better if she called me. But what if she didn't? Outside of Sean, Kick was the only person who knew about me. She was the only one I wanted to be with now. Well, almost the only one.

. . .

Sitting in homeroom on Monday, I scanned the front page of the *Whitman Journal*. The top headline read "After-Finals Bash Set for December 21." I wanted to go.

I found Kick at her locker after homeroom. The way she drew in a breath made me feel like an intruder.

"Hey," I said, watching her as she shoved math and history books into her backpack. She nodded at me and started walking. I followed. "What's up?"

"Nothing," she said. We navigated through the crowded hallways. Usually, Kick would be talking nonstop. But today, silence.

I walked her to history class. "Are you mad? Seems like you are."

"Nope," she said, disappearing inside.

The next few days were the same. Kick wasn't hostile, but I didn't get the impression she wanted me around. I had so many things to tell her. But the more I tried to be close, the more distant she seemed.

After school, I picked up a makeup assignment from Detweiler. As he explained what I had to do, I noticed he had a poster in rainbow colors: "Diversity Is Our Strength."

School had cleared out by the time I left. Going to my locker, I saw Eddie down the hall, tacking a poster onto the student-activities board. Rick Cutter and Brad Morte came around the corner, saw Eddie, and stopped. Cutter bumped into him. "You're turning this into Homo High," he accused. I ducked inside an empty classroom, peeking out to watch.

"Could you move!" Eddie demanded. Cutter was crowding him.

"Shut up!" Brad cuffed Eddie's head. Rick took the Gay/Straight Alliance poster and ripped it in half.

"Stop it," Eddie said. "You can't do that."

Cutter ripped the poster into confetti. "Fairy dust," he said.

Brad jammed his elbow into Eddie's ribs. Then they ran off, their laughter echoing behind them down the long hallway.

I rushed to see if Eddie was okay. He didn't look at me, his eyes fixed on the French-club poster. He ripped it down. "What are you doing?" I asked as he tore it in half. He pulled down the notice for drama tryouts and the Career Day poster.

"Eddie, don't." I tacked one of the posters back up.

"ASSHOLES!" he shouted down the hallway, clutching his side.

He turned back to me. "How can I get people to the meetings," he asked, "if they tear down my posters?"

"You can make more."

"I can't even get *you* to the meetings," he said, "and you're gay."

"What?"

"Give it up, I know."

I dug my fingernails into the flesh of my palms. "Who told you that?"

"No one *had* to tell me. I've known it as long as I've known about me. Are you ever coming out? I mean, in this lifetime?" Eddie stared at me.

"That's not your business."

"Yeah, it is. Since you started ignoring me because I'm gay."

"That's not it. You like making a scene," I whispered. "It's embarrassing."

"What?!" Eddie flung half a poster at me. "At least I don't abandon my friends."

"Neither do I."

"Not if they're rich. And straight."

"Is that what you think?"

"It's true, isn't it?"

I marched off, furious that Eddie had made me feel bad about myself. He had a way of doing that.

Slush from last weekend's snowfall lined the streets as I headed home. This had to be Kick's fault. Sworn to secrecy only three days ago, she'd already betrayed me. My stomach burned.

I cut across the street just as a whole line of cars came shooting around the curve. Leaping for the sidewalk on the other side, I landed one foot in a deep pile of slush. Icy water poured into my shoe. I screamed. Everything was fucked!

CHAPTER

TWENTY-FIVE

I was lying crosswise on my bed, head and legs jutting off, my sock still wet from the slush puddle, when my phone rang.

"David, I'm sorry." Kick sounded plaintive. Eddie must have called her. "You know how Eddie gets things out of people. I couldn't take it back."

"Kick! You promised NOT TO TELL."

"It's true, I did."

"You have a big mouth."

"I know. I have to work on myself."

"Work on yourself? I'd say so."

"David, don't be mad. I'm sorry."

"Don't ever—EVER—tell another person."

"I swear to God I won't."

"Not that it matters—since Eddie knows, everyone will." I hung up before she could say another word.

Now, how would I stop the Mouth of Minnesota?

My heart began pounding. Was I having a panic attack? I took deep breaths as my heart raced. There was only one way to calm myself. I tore off my clothes and put on my running suit. It was cold and snowy. But I didn't care. I had to run.

The world outside was so quiet, with snow muffling the city noise. I ran along Minnehaha Parkway to Lake Nokomis, passing snow-dusted shaggy green pines. The cold air hitting my face made me run faster. I could feel my body, moving, straining, letting go. And then I hit that spot. A feeling of oneness came over me. The trees, the sky, the snow. Nothing could touch me now.

"You're quiet," Mom said as we finished dinner that night.

I shrugged. Truth was, I was feeling bad about Eddie.

"Well, help me with these dishes, quiet one."

"Okay," I said, taking the dish towel. It was nice standing there with her, drying. She knew I didn't want to talk and let me be.

I waited until Mom was deep into her medical drama that night before I went to my room, closed the door, and dialed the hotline number. "Hi, Jim," I said quietly when he answered. It's me, um . . . Bob."

"How ya doin'?"

"Not so good, really."

"What's wrong?"

I wondered if Jim could hear how loudly I was swallowing. "How come some people hate gays so much?"

"What makes you say that?"

I told him what happened to Eddie, trembling as I recounted it. "Why did they go after him?"

"They feel threatened."

"They do?"

"Sure. They have to prove something. That they're super-masculine guys."

I kept seeing Morte's elbow gouging into Eddie's side. "Do you think I'm a coward for just standing there?"

"No."

"I do."

"It was a volatile situation."

"I hid until they were gone."

"Is Eddie all right?"

"I think so."

"We can't all be Aaron Fricke," Jim said.

"Who's that?"

"He took a guy to his high-school prom. In 1980, mind you. And then he wrote a book about it."

"He took a guy to his prom? As his date?"

"Yup."

"Did they dance together?"

"Uh-huh. At first, everyone stared at them. But before long, people joined them on the dance floor. You should read the book. *Reflections of a Rock Lobster.*"

"Can I get it online?"

"Yes. But where do you live?"

"Minneapolis."

"There is a great bookstore there, the Amazon Bookstore Cooperative, where you'll find it. A visit will do you good."

David wrote it down. Then the switchboard flooded with calls, and Jim had to go.

"You'll be there next Wednesday, right?" I asked.

"Mmhmm."

"Okay if I keep calling?"

"Look forward to it, Bob."

"Oh, umm . . . my name's really David."

"Oh. I'm glad you told me, David."

"Me too."

After I got off the phone, I told Mom I was going for a drive. Pretending that I was just aimlessly heading up and down the blocks around Lake Calhoun, I knew where the car would end up. I shut off the ignition and glided silently into a spot across the street. Downstairs, the house was dark, but his bedroom light was on.

I imagined Sean, dressed in a tuxedo, picking me up to drive to the prom. When we arrived, the room would buzz as everyone realized we had come together. We'd be caught up with dancing and laughing all night. Our lives would be changed forever, just like Aaron Fricke's.

Only Fricke really did it. I looked up at Sean's bedroom window again. I might do it, but he never would.

CHAPTER

TWENTY-SIX

"Bye, Mom," I called up the stairs as I left for school.

"David, have you got a hat?"

I slipped out the front door without one, went down the steps, and crossed the dead lawn crusted with ice. None of the guys at Whitman wore hats, no matter how far below zero it got.

The December landscape was bleak, mud-brown. All the snow had melted. I longed to be back in my bed. For too long now, the best part of each day was falling asleep. But it always came time to get up again, to walk past lifeless trees, to slump into my desk at school. In English I would see Sean. His clipped hellos and empty eyes were like sweat in a paper cut.

The truth was, I missed Eddie. I flipped open my cell phone and hit his number. Then I hung up. I didn't know what to say.

That Saturday, I drove to a place I had been wanting to go to for days but had been too scared. I sat for a long time watching the door. Two women went in. Then a guy. A man came out, pulled on a red stocking cap, and walked up the street.

I didn't want to leave my car. But why come here if I wasn't going in?

This was the place. The Amazon Bookstore Cooperative that Jim had told me about. So comfortably situated on Chicago Avenue. No one paying it any mind. That was the great thing about Minneapolis. All the Swedes and Norwegians. They minded their own business. The wind's cold arms found their way down my jacket, making me shiver and hurry inside.

The store was filled with people browsing, mostly women. Were they all lesbians? Would they think I was gay? I edged my way into the store.

"Have you got, um, *Reflections of a Rock Lobster*?" I asked at the cash register.

The clerk pointed over my head. "The section on coming out. Next to Parenting."

Parenting? As I walked through that section, I saw two women holding hands.

I found Fricke's book. Down the aisle, two men were talking.

"Come over later," one said as he browsed through the small collection of DVDs. "Juan-Carlos and Ilan will be there. And the Bills." He pulled out a movie. "After dinner, we're going to watch *My Beautiful Laundrette*."

"Oh, Daniel Day-Lewis is incredible in that."

"So, we'll see you later?"

I scurried away before they noticed me eavesdropping. As the clerk rang up my purchases he asked if I wanted a schedule of events at the store. Shaking my head without thinking, I later wished I'd taken it. For a few moments, Whitman seemed so far away. Maybe there was life outside high school.

I sat in the car, using the penlight on my key chain to read the first chapter of my book. The two men I had seen talking walked out of the bookstore. They seemed so nice. I wanted to go to their party.

After school on Monday, a note fell out on me when I opened my locker. Oh, God, not another one of these. I tore it open, recognizing Kick's handwriting.

Dear David,

I probably shouldn't even write. But you know how I am. Boy, do you!

For most of this year I have felt closer to you than any other guy. Which is saying a lot, because I am shy around boys (even though no one can believe that). It took me a long time to crack through your reserve. But finally I did.

I was hurt when you told me about yourself. But I've gotten over that. I understand why you're mad that I told Eddie. I just don't know how to change it.

When I see you now, it feels like you're miles

away. Maybe that's the way it has to be. I hope not. Because sometimes you look sad.

Anyway, what I'm trying to say is, isn't there some way we could be friends again?

Love,

Kick

Jamming the note into my shirt pocket, I raced down the hallway to the back exit from school. Maybe I could still catch her.

Slap! I hit the bar release and shot out of the building. Her car was just leaving. "KICK!" The red Volvo turned left onto Fiftieth. "KICK!" I sprinted after her.

My only chance was the stop sign at the end of the block. I poured it on. As she rolled to a stop, I slapped her bumper. "GOTCHA."

Completely oblivious, she accelerated, barreling through the intersection and out of my reach, leaving me breathing heavily, shaking my head.

Kick didn't answer her phone when I tried to call, so I went home and sent her a short e-mail: "Still want to be friends. That was never a question. D."

I headed outside for a bicycle ride. Without thinking about it, I ended up on Eddie's block. He was out front brushing Shirley. I stopped and hopped off my bike.

"Hey, Eddie."

"Well, look who's here." Eddie pulled a handful of blond hair out of his brush and threw it on the lawn. "Got a flat?"

"Hey, give me some credit."

"Why?"

"Cause I'm trying."

"A little late."

I put down the kickstand, and Shirley ran to me. Grabbing the dog, I pulled her close. Shirley licked my lips. "Stop!" I commanded. Eddie laughed. Pulling Shirley back to him, I said, "I've had a hard time too, you know."

"Oh, you poor thing."

"Look, I'm sorry."

"Saying you're sorry is not a cure-all," he replied, skewering me with my own words from long ago. Eddie turned back to Shirley. I watched him brush her for a minute or two, and when he didn't look up, I took off. This was going to be harder than I thought.

CHAPTER

TWENTY-SEVEN

My cell woke me from a sound sleep Saturday morning.

"Huh?" I rubbed my eyes and looked at the clock. Eleven a.m. Cold air rushed over my bare chest as I reached for the phone. "Hello," I croaked.

"I woke you," Kick said.

"Not really." I was glad to hear from her.

"Go back to sleep."

"No, I'm up now. What's going on?"

"I'm trying to find someone to go with me to the cabin."

"This time of year?"

"It's a perfect place to study," she said. "Finals are coming up. You want to go? We'll come back tomorrow."

"Yeah, sure."

"How soon can you be ready?"

I sniffed at my armpit. "An hour?"

"Good. I'll pick you up."

After I was dressed and packed, I found Mom in the kitchen. She watched me as I sliced a banana onto a bowl of cereal. "I'm going to Kick's cabin for the weekend," I said breezily, splashing milk on the cereal. "Up on Lake Mille Lacs."

"This is the first I'm hearing of it." She sat down with her coffee and gave me a skeptical look. "Who's going?"

"Just me," I said, spooning the cereal into my mouth, "and Kick."

"What about her parents?"

"I didn't ask them what they're doing."

"Do they know about this?"

"Yeah, definitely." I was sure Kick had told them.

There was silence, and I could feel her eyes on my face. Did she have any idea about me?

"Kick's parents don't mind her spending the weekend alone with a boy?"

I shrugged. "We're just friends."

"I thought you were dating."

"Mom. It's not like 1970 anymore. Kids my age don't date."

"What do they do?"

"I don't know. But whatever it is, Kick and I aren't doing it. So, can I go? Please?"

She picked up the phone. "What's Kick's number? I'll speak to her mother."

"NO! Mom, why do you have to make it embarrassing for me?"

She shook her head and hung up. "This is against my better judgment."

"We'll be fine."

"Will I be able to reach you?"

"Kick gave me the cabin number," I said, writing it down on her grocery list. Our cell phones probably wouldn't work up there.

BEEP! BEEP! Kick was honking out front. I jumped up and grabbed my packed knapsack.

"Wait. When will you be back?"

"Tomorrow."

"I want you home by eight o'clock. David? Agreed?"

"Yes." I ran down the driveway and got in the car. Kick and I waved to my mother as we drove off.

"You rescued me," I told her.

"From what?"

"Prying questions."

"Oh?"

"She wanted to know what your parents thought of us going away together."

"She did?" I nodded. "My parents didn't care," Kick said. "Not after I told them you were gay."

"WHAT!"

"Kidding. I'm kidding. They think I'm going with Mona. So don't answer the phone this weekend." I laughed and sank back into the bucket seat. As we drove, Kick played the radio loudly and told me the latest things her mother had done that made Kick crazy. Like limiting her cell-phone minutes so she'd study more. After a long stretch on the freeway, we turned onto country roads. Static came over the radio more than music, and I turned it off. We drove in silence as the landscape outside the car became forested. Finally, we turned into a long driveway lined thick with evergreens. "Here we are," Kick said as she jangled her keys.

The cabin looked as if made of Lincoln Logs. Inside was one big room, paneled in knotty pine. A white enamel sink and stove stood on one end and a stone fireplace on the other. The two tiny bedrooms barely held the double beds.

"Is this place heated?" I asked, watching my breath form into clouds.

"Mmhmm." Kick nodded, turning up the thermostat on the wall. "And the fireplace works great."

"I should call my mom."

"There's the phone." I dialed, got the answering machine, and told her we'd arrived safely.

As Kick called her mom, I wandered down to the shore. Lake Mille Lacs was huge, surrounded by stands of red pine and Norway spruce. Tiny cabins dotted the landscape.

Back inside, Kick was sprawled on the couch, reading *Siddhartha*.

"What page are you on?" I asked, pulling out my copy.

"Forty-nine."

"I'm only on thirty-two."

"Well, get going," she admonished me. "We have to discuss it before Monday."

When dusk settled on the lake, Kick got up and switched on lamps made of pinecones. "Do you like spaghetti hot dish?" she asked.

"Sure." Whatever that was, it sounded good.

Kick began browning hamburger in a cast-iron skillet, joining it with a large container of canned spaghetti. My mouth watered. While the spaghetti bubbled, she spread garlic butter onto hotdog buns and browned them under the broiler.

"Yum. I'm starving."

"Make a fire. Then we'll eat."

The flames were blazing by the time Kick put two steaming plates on the table. "I don't think my dad would miss a bottle of Beaujolais, do you?" she asked, uncorking it.

I took a long sip of the mellow wine and gorged on the heaping plate of pasta. "So good," I said, between crunches of the garlicky toast. "When did you learn to cook?" Kick just smiled.

After I had downed the last morsel of hot dish, Kick disappeared into the bedroom, saying she wanted to get cozy. She came back in a long nightshirt with Tweety Bird on it and stretched out on the braided rug. I dropped down next to her. Popping and hissing, blue fingers of flame curled around the logs. My head tingled with wine. "I love being with you," I said.

"You do?" Kick's toes wiggled against mine.

"Yeah. I don't have to pretend."

"About what?"

"I can say how I really feel about Sean."

Kick pulled her foot back. "How?"

"I love him." Tears filled my eyes. "And he won't even talk

to me." I didn't know it was going to happen then. But it did. My chest started heaving, and I sobbed. Everything that had built up over months decided at that moment to come out. She moved over and put her arm around me. But that just made me cry more. Poor Kick must have wondered if I was having a breakdown right there in her cabin.

"It's okay, David," she said.

I finally quieted down, exhausted, but feeling better. I got up, went into the bathroom, and blew my nose.

Kick followed me in. "What happened with you two anyway?"

We went back, sat in front of the fire, and I told her everything: the note, the sex (well, there I didn't tell everything), his evil mother, and now his "straight" regimen.

Kick took a piece of kindling and poked at the embers. "How long are you going to wait for him to come back?"

I shrugged. Is that what I was doing?

Kick stood and got the wine. "Should we kill this?"

"Sure."

She divided the last of it into our two glasses. Staring at the fire, we let its flicker hypnotize us. When the flames began to die down, I tossed in another log. A spray of glowing orange sparks shot up the chimney like a comet's tail. "Is there more wood?"

Kick nodded. "Around back."

Slipping shoes on my feet, I ducked outside. The air was sharp and cold. I pulled split logs from the pile and headed back into the cabin. Sitting cross-legged in front of the fire, listening to the whisper of the flames, I felt Kick's warm hand on my neck. "Ooh, you're cold." She rubbed her hands over my back.

"That feels good," I said, easing down onto the floor, suddenly woozy.

She rubbed my shoulders and then curled up behind me, front pressed to my back. "Is this okay?" she asked.

"Mmhmmm." As we lay there nestled together, Kick started to my play with my hair. "David?" she said. "This may sound crazy."

"What?"

"I was thinking, maybe, you know, you would want to experiment tonight." Every cell of my body froze. Kick brought her lips near my ear. "I'm not a virgin, you know."

"You're not?" I sat up and took a gulp of wine.

"Not since last summer."

"Tell me."

"Well . . . Mona and I met these two guys from Marshall U High School. At the band shell on Lake Harriet. They were watching us. You know Mona—she loves black guys. So off we went to talk to them."

"They were black?"

"Yeah. So Mona makes a play for the taller one, Rufus. And pretty soon we're driving around the lake in their car. I was in back with Jamal, thinking I'm going to kill Mona. But it turns out he's really sweet. He starts telling me how sexy I am. And I'm like, Yeah, right."

"Oh, Kick."

"He says I'm voluptuous."

"Well, you are."

"It goes along with being fat. Well, anyway, over the next couple of weeks we start seeing these guys every night. Going to Rudolphs, shooting pool, driving around a lot. And then one day Mona says Rufus is having a party and that I should tell my parents I'm staying over at her house. It turns out to be a big party. Jamal and I end up in a bedroom and . . . that's the night it happened."

"How was it?"

"He knew what he was doing."

"So, what happened to Jamal? You never mentioned him before."

"He left for college. I got a few e-mails, but that was it. I'm sure he has another girlfriend now." Kick got up. "Don't move, I have to pee."

As Kick disappeared into the bathroom, I wondered what it would feel like with a girl. Shouldn't I try it at least once? But would I be as good as Jamal? Kick came back, and I nestled against her. Lying there in front of the fire, we held each other.

She started kissing the back of my neck. As I turned to her, she pursed her lips in the glow of the crackling fire. I kissed them. Wanting to. The more we kissed, the more I wanted it. The soft, sensuous touch of her lips excited me.

We took a rest to catch our breath, and Kick whispered in my ear. "After I'm under the covers you come in, all right?" She was gone.

I waited, noticing my rapid breath. Reaching down, to make sure life was there, I felt proud.

"Okay," Kick called from behind the closed door of the bedroom.

I pulled off my sweatshirt and slowly entered the dark room. "Hi, there," she said quietly as I slipped under the covers. "What are these?" Kick asked, brushing my leg.

"Sweatpants."

"I'm not wearing anything." She giggled, tugging at my pants.

I slid out of them, and our naked bodies came together. She was warm everywhere.

"Ohhh." Kick sighed. I buried my face in the nape of her neck, my eyes tightly closed. Kick felt soft, pudgy, not lean and hard like Sean. We started kissing. I put my tongue into her mouth, and she sucked it in deeper. But my hard-on was gone.

Kick slipped down and went to work. I could feel my face turning red in the dark. Nothing was happening. What did I do now? My stomach sank. Should I say something? But I couldn't talk. This was too weird.

I focused my mind on running. The soft thud of feet. The breath in my ear. His breath. His touch. My reverie had results.

She scooted up, reached under her pillow, and handed me a tinfoil package. "Here."

I got the condom on and crawled back under the covers.

"You okay?" Kick asked.

"Mmhmm," I said, wondering if this was a mistake.

She pulled me on top of her, and I felt her guiding me into place. Her breath came sharp. I knew what to do now. As my body moved, up and back, I imagined looking down from the ceiling upon our strange gyrations. Kick's fingernails dug into me, then she raised her hips as I kept pumping. There was friction. Which did its job. I came. "Oh, baby," Kick said.

I got up, wanting air.

"Where are you going?"

"Bathroom." Inside the john, I closed the door, glad to be alone for a minute. The light hurt my eyes. Looking in the mirror, I mouthed: "Now you know."

Out in the living room, the embers slowly died in the fireplace. I crawled back into bed with sweats on. Kick eased herself closer to me, resting her arm across my bare chest. It had been so nice with Kick in front of the fire. Why did I feel so lonely now?

CHAPTER

TWENTY-EIGHT

Feeling a presence, I stirred from my sleep. Kick was looming over me. "Breakfast in bed," she cooed. The tray she set down on the quilt next to me held a plate with two fried eggs. Their yellow yolks, drizzled in ketchup, stared up at me like blood-shot eyes. Suddenly nauseous, I groaned and turned over. "Oh, all right, sleepy." She lifted the tray off the bed and left the room, humming.

Another hour went by before I hauled myself out of bed and slumped into the rocker in front of the fireplace. Sitting down next to me on the floor, Kick started rubbing my foot. I pulled both legs up under me.

"You need aspirin?"

"I'm okay."

"Want the eggs now?"

"No food yet. When are we going home?"

"I wish we could stay another night."

I was ready to go. The rush of the wind in the eaves made me look out. Dried leaves scratched across the bare ground. "Nasty out there."

Kick reached up and rubbed her hand across my thigh. "You cold?"

I pushed her hand away. "Stop it."

"What? Is that so bad?" She turned around to face me. "We're more than friends now, you know."

"I thought you said we were experimenting."

She studied my face. "Didn't you like it?"

I glanced out the window and then turned back to Kick. "Yeah. Sort of. But it didn't really do anything for me." She stared at me, blinking hard, and then ran into the bedroom, shutting the door behind her.

"Kick," I called to her. Silence. The door flew open. She didn't look at me or say a word as she pulled on her ski jacket and rushed down the back steps. "Where are you going?" I called after her. Without answering, she fled up the driveway, turning past the Norway spruce out onto the main road.

I fell back into the rocker.

Just then, the ring of the phone made me jump. I walked over to the wall, reached for it, and then remembered Kick telling me not to answer. It felt funny to be all alone in Kick's cabin. As I stood there, snowflakes began flying past the window, small at first and then bigger and bigger. The ground was soon dusted in white. I went outside.

Peering through the thick air, I tried to catch a glimpse of Kick. Wet flakes landed on my eyelashes. I ran and skidded across the slippery ground in my street shoes a few times. Pretending to have fun.

It was past lunchtime, and I was getting hungry. Inside,

the uneaten eggs sat there, as if to reproach me. I snacked on leftover garlic bread and American-cheese singles. Where the hell did Kick go?

Standing in front of the window, I watched the snow fall relentlessly, piling up on the ground inch by inch. We had to get out of here soon. Was Kick lost?

I had decided to go out looking, when the cabin door opened and Kick stomped in. Her hair glistened white, and the shoulders of her coat were covered.

"Where were you?"

She shook the snow out of her hair and brushed off her jacket. "Walking."

"We better get going or we'll be snowed in."

"So, did you do the dishes?" She waved her hand over the mess in the kitchen. "Are you packed?"

The telephone started ringing again, and Kick grabbed it.

"Hello." She put her hand over the mouthpiece and whispered to me, "It's my mother." Then she spoke into the phone. "We're packing now. Leaving any minute." Pause. "I told you," she said into the phone. "Mona." Kick gave me a panicked look. "What did you call her parents for? God, I hate when you check up on me."

Kick let out a groan. "Okay, it's David. Big deal." I could hear her mom's voice coming out of the phone.

"Stop yelling at me. We have to pack and go. Do you want us stranded up here?" Kick started crying. "I will. Okay. Yes, I'll drive slowly." She hung up and ran to the bathroom.

I finished the dishes, closed the fireplace flue, and packed my things. Then Kick came out, her eyes all puffy. She stripped the bed, and I helped her put clean sheets on.

"I'm sorry, Kick."

"Me too."

I loaded the car as Kick closed up inside. Four o'clock and it was already dusk. The snow kept coming down through the whistling wind.

Kick locked the cabin and got in behind the wheel. Inching slowly out of the driveway, she turned onto the roadway. Snowflakes flew at us in the high beams. "I can't see," she said.

"You're doing fine. Just go slow."

Kick grew braver as we went along, gradually increasing her speed as she squinted to see. Suddenly, something sprang into the road ahead of us. A deer.

"Stop!" I yelled.

Kick slammed on the brakes. The car skidded. Kick lost control and careened off the road. My body was thrown against the door as we bounced to a stop.

"Oh my God!" Kick cried.

"Are you okay?" I asked, rubbing my shoulder.

"I think so." We climbed out of the Volvo, which was hopelessly marooned in the drainage ditch. "It's five miles back to the cabin," Kick said. She started pushing all the buttons on her cell phone, but couldn't get a signal.

I looked around for lights from a house. But all I could see were thick evergreens and the whipping snow.

CHAPTER

TWENTY-NINE

Snowflakes bit at my face in the fierce wind. I zipped up my parka and pulled on gloves. "Where are we?"

Kick looked unsure. "I think there's a little town, Giese, up that way." She pointed at snow swirling in the blackness.

"How far?" She shrugged. The wind howled in the trees behind us.

"Let's get back in the car," Kick said.

We climbed in, and Kick started the engine. "Thank God. Heat."

"What's our plan?" I asked.

"Somebody will come by," Kick said confidently, putting on the emergency flashers. We sat quietly for ten minutes, twenty, a half hour. No one came by.

"What if they don't?" I asked.

Kick shrugged. "Guess we sleep in the car."

"I'll try to find a house," I said. "We haven't even looked."

I started off in the driving storm, just sweat socks and loafers on my feet. The snow, shin-deep now, slipped into my shoes, melting against my skin. I sank with each step, so my progress was slow. My lungs strained like they did near the end of a race.

The falling, blowing snow seemed to erase the world. I kept going in the darkness, but came upon nothing except the silhouettes of trees. My face was raw from the constant wind. I had to get back to the car.

I turned and retraced my footprints, already half-filled. My toes were numb by the time I saw the stranded Volvo, gradually disappearing into the whiteness. I ran, pulled open the door, and jumped into the warmth. "Find anything?" Kick asked.

I shook my head, pulling off my wet socks and shoving my bare feet up against the warm stream of air blowing from the heater.

"We don't have much gas," she told me.

"What? Turn it off. We'll need the heater later." Kick switched off the car and it shuddered to a stop. She turned off the emergency flashers.

My feet started to itch. I yanked them up inside my sweatpants and massaged my toes. Kick cracked the door open every few minutes to listen for a car or a snowplow.

"Look on the bright side," I said to her. "At least we won't have school tomorrow."

"One more day I don't have to see my mother," she replied.

A half hour passed. The cold slowly penetrated. My fingers hurt. I started shivering. "Kick, let's run the heater again."

She turned the ignition. Nothing happened. She tried

again. It ground and ground without turning over. "Keep trying!" I said. "Pump the gas." She turned the key. Nothing. She kept trying. But the longer she ground the engine the less it responded. And then, only clicking.

It was ten hours to daylight.

I opened my door. "HELP!" I shouted into the swirling void. "ANYBODY!"

"You're scaring me," Kick said. A blast of icy wind and snow hit my face. With clumsy fingers, I pulled the door closed. "Kick, I can't feel my toes anymore."

"Let's put on all our clothes," she said, suddenly hopping out into the snow. I heard her brushing snow off the tail of the car. Kick came back and popped the trunk.

"David!" she cried. "My little brother's sleeping bag!"

I stared at the maroon bundle Kick shoved at me. "Kirby, I love you!"

I climbed in back, and Kick gave me the bag to lay out. "We should take our clothes off and both get in," I told her.

"Why?"

"To keep each other warm with our body heat."

Kick was quiet for a minute.

"Kick! This is about staying alive." Soon I was inside, naked except for my boxers. I let my hot breath rush into the bag. "Feels better already."

Kick climbed into the back. She undressed, except for her underwear, and I opened the sleeping bag for her. She slid in hurriedly, pressed her back against me, and zippered us shut.

"Oh, you're warm," I said, curling my feet up and putting them against her legs.

"Aayyhh!" she screamed. "Your toes are like ice." But she held them there between her calves. My toes started to ache and itch as the warmth of her body brought feeling back into them.

I pressed my face against Kick's back and hugged her to me. We passed the time playing Twenty Questions and talking about who would be up for Winter Solstice King and Queen. Then, zipped together in one cocoon, exhaustion overtook us and we slept.

I don't know how long I'd been asleep when a scraping sound woke me. It was still night. Headlights were fixed on our car. Snow fell from the window, swept away by a blue bristled brush. A face peered in. Kick stirred, looked up, and gasped. "Oh my God, it's Daddy!"

CHAPTER

THIRTY

Kick seized my corduroy shirt from the floor and slapped it against the window. "Get dressed!" she hissed. I unzipped us and grabbed for my jeans.

"Kick! You okay?" her father shouted, rapping on the window. Elbows and knees collided as we scrambled to get dressed in the tilting car. While I helped Kick slide into her pants, her father scraped off the window on the other side of the car. I shoved the sleeping bag up against the glass. "Get your pants on," Kick commanded as she struggled into her sweatshirt.

Kick wriggled her feet into her boots, slid out of the car, and slammed the door behind her. Holding the sleeping bag against the window with my feet, I hiked up my jeans. Just as I hooked the top button, Mr. Shapiro yanked open the door.

He steadied his gaze on me as I lay on the seat, shirtless. "Get in the Jeep."

I finished dressing and climbed out. A police cruiser flashed its red lights. Kick tried to mouth something to me as her father marched us to his vehicle, but I couldn't get what it was.

Mr. Shapiro took Kick's hand once we were inside his four-wheel drive. "Thank God, you're alive. The police were out looking for you. Your mother's been worried sick. And so has yours, David." He stared back at me. "She called last night, and we didn't know what to tell her." The Jeep lurched into gear, and we roared off through the unplowed snow. Kick and I didn't dare speak.

When we got closer to the city, Mr. Shapiro called Kick's mother on the cell and told her we were safe. Then he told me to call my mother. She picked up on the first ring. All night she had worried about me. "Sorry, Mom," I told her. She sounded more relieved than angry.

"What's going to happen to my car?" Kick asked.

"We'll tow it to the cabin," her father said.

"When can we get it?"

"Next spring," he said firmly.

"Spring! But Daddy, how will I get around?"

"You aren't going *anywhere.*" Kick looked back at me miserably.

It was a long ride back to the city without conversation.

As they dropped me off at home, Kick seemed really down. She barely said good-bye. I guess losing your car for the whole winter in Minnesota pretty much sucks. Not to mention our little bedroom escapade. And the fact we almost froze.

Making it to the front door of my house, all ten toes still attached, I looked up. "Thank you, God," I whispered, vowing that I would start going to church every Sunday.

Mom was waiting inside for me in her robe, dark rings under her eyes. She looked hard at me. "I was up all night."

"I'm sorry." I threw my arms around her. Tears welled in my eyes. Mom hugged me back.

"I should have called Kick's parents before you went up there," she said, stepping back and looking at me. "Like I wanted to. They didn't know she was up there with you."

"I thought she told them." I made a pleading face. "We couldn't help what happened."

"David, if I ever lost you . . ."

"You won't, Mom."

Upstairs, turning the thermostat up to eighty-five degrees, I fell into bed and wrapped the quilt around me. Under the covers, I rubbed my bare feet, now warm. It was good to be alive.

THIRTY-ONE

Even though I begged to stay home in bed on Tuesday, Mom said one day off was enough. The look on her face meant there wasn't any arguing. At least she drove me on her way to the U.

Harvey Gersh grilled me in physics lab. "So? Where were you yesterday?"

"Up north."

"Yeah? Why didn't you make it back?"

"Got caught in the blizzard."

"You and Kick?" Harvey smirked.

"Yeah."

"Did you get in her pants?"

I flinched. "None of your business."

"You did!" He nudged me with his shoulder. "Tell me."

"I'm not telling you anything."

"Why?"

"You'll spread it around."

"Me?" Harvey drew back. "It might be good for you if I did."

"What's that supposed to mean?"

"Heard a rumor about you." He flopped his wrist in mocking imitation. The muscles in my jaw tightened. "You're not that way, are you?" Harvey looked at me intently.

I could feel the pulse in my temples. "What if I am?"

"I want a new lab partner."

I shook my head. "Don't be a jerk."

Was I that obvious?

When I ran into Kick at school that week she was always with someone or in a hurry. We never got to talk. I kept hoping she would call or e-mail me, but a week went by and she didn't return the messages I left on her cell.

Thursday, I e-mailed her. No reply. Friday, after school, I gave in and called her landline. Her little brother answered. "Hey, Kirby, how ya doing?"

I heard the phone clunk down. "KICK!" he shouted. "It's your BOYFRIEND!" I waited for a long time, and then Kick came on.

"What are you doing tonight?" I asked.

"I'm not allowed to leave the house."

"I could come over."

Pause. "Thanks, but I don't think so."

"Tomorrow night?"

"David, don't you get it?"

"What?"

"I need some time. Away from you."

"Oh."

"Okay?"

"Yeah, I understand."

"I'll see you around school," she said, and hung up.

"Bye," I said to the disconnected line. So, now my one real friend was off-limits?

I needed Mom. She was putting on makeup in her bedroom and smiled at me in the mirror. I watched her color her lips deep red, then blot them with a tissue. "You and Rosie going out tonight?" I asked.

"No." My mother met my eyes. "I have a date."

"You do?" Dating and my mother were not even remotely connected. "Who with?"

"Someone I met at the faculty party."

"You got picked up?"

She laughed. "We hit it off, and he called me, that's all." She started to jab at her hair with a brush. "What are you doing tonight?"

"Nothin'."

She turned and looked at me, puzzled. "Staying in on a Friday night?"

"Finals start Monday."

"Okay, there's meat loaf for your dinner. Microwave it for two minutes."

The doorbell rang. She put her compact into her purse and gave me a quick, one-armed hug. "Love you," she whispered into my ear and then hurried down the stairs. I plopped on my bed, listening to her greet her date.

When hunger pangs hit me, I went downstairs, pulled out the meat loaf, and ate a big hunk cold with my fingers, standing in front of the fridge. Then I made a chocolate-banana milkshake, dragged the quilt from my bed into the den upstairs, and plopped onto the floor.

I put on the film I rented, *Sleepless in Seattle*. If I only had someone to watch it with.

Meg Ryan was getting ever nearer to Tom Hanks when I heard the doorbell ring. That was odd. Maybe Mrs. Timothy locked herself out again. I bounded down the stairs. Frost covered the storm door so I couldn't see. I unlatched it and pushed it open. And there he stood. The last person in the world I expected on my doorstep.

Sean.

CHAPTER

THIRTY-TWO

"How are ya?" he asked, taking me in with an innocent look, as if he hadn't been ignoring me for weeks. "Can I come in?" The smell of beer hit me as he stepped through the door. Spreading the afghan over the frayed edges of the couch, I motioned for him to sit down.

"Hungry?" I asked, darting into the kitchen. What was he doing here! I grabbed a box of Chicken In A Biskit crackers and poured them out on a plate.

"Crackers?" I offered, setting the plate onto the coffee table. I reached for a handful and began eating them rapid-fire.

"We're not staying here," he said.

I swallowed. "Where we going?"

Sean shrugged.

"I have to change," I said, tugging on my sweatpants.

Upstairs, pulling on jeans and a turtleneck, I thought: Am I crazy? Going off in the car with Sean? I sat down on the bed. A voice inside my head shouted warnings.

Then he appeared in my room. Lanky with his bright blue eyes. I tucked in my shirt.

"Looks good," he said, rubbing his hand down the front of it. I caught his hand and pushed it away. "Should we go?" I asked nervously. Sean turned and walked through my doorway.

"Let's just drive," he said when we reached the car. He bent his tall frame to fit into the sedan.

I climbed in next to him and buckled up. Why did I feel a crash was coming? As he headed toward downtown Minneapolis, we chatted about stupid stuff like commercials and movies we didn't want to see. Sean smiled at me like a horny sailor.

Neon lights came into view. "Look. The Go-Go Girls strip bar," Sean pointed as we turned off Hennepin onto First Avenue. "Want to see some pussy?"

"Not really," I replied.

"I know what you want to see." Sean looked at me and grinned.

He put jazz on the radio, and we cruised. I tried to collect my thoughts.

Sean drove across the Mississippi on the Washington Avenue Bridge to St. Anthony Main, a shopping center that never really made it. Asphalt gave way to the old cobblestone streets that had served the grain warehouses. The car bumped over the uneven road, and Sean let it glide to a stop.

It was dark. He undid his seat belt and looked at me.

I wanted to say something, to talk to him, but found no words.

Unzipping, he lifted his hips off the seat. I shoved his thighs down, yanked open the door, and ran toward the river.

"Where you going?" Sean called out his window.

I kept running.

He chased me. Coming upon a footbridge, I dropped down onto the narrow wooden structure and let my legs hang over. Patches of unmelted snow on the riverbank glistened in the light of the half moon. Sean pulled a beer out of his jacket, flipped the top, and handed it to me. "Thanks," I said, taking a gulp.

He sat down next to me, pressing his leg against mine.

"You still seeing your shrink?" I asked.

"Yeah."

"What's it like?"

Sean looked off in the distance. "He asks me all these questions. To find out if I'm nuts, I guess."

"Like what?"

"What do I dream about? What's my first memory?" Sean opened a beer. "And of course, sexual stuff. Boy, does he love to talk about that."

"Did you tell him about me?"

"My mom did."

"Oh, great!"

"Don't worry, my shrink doesn't give a shit what she thinks. He makes fun of her."

"Maybe he's okay."

"He asked me if you were a nice person. He wanted to know if you did drugs. And then he asked me why I stopped being friends with you. The thing is, he's always asking me what I want."

"Which is what?"

"You mean right this minute?" Sean rubbed his hand down the back of my head, causing the hairs on my neck to stand up. He unbuttoned the waist of his jeans.

I looked around nervously. Wasn't this against the law? Sean stood up.

My heart pounded. I playfully bit his thigh. And then I stood up too.

"Sit down," he urged.

I shook my head and ran back to the street.

As we got into the car, I pointed to a squad car up the street. Sean hit the accelerator too hard and we skidded out. He drove to the White Castle on University Avenue. We ate sixteen sliders between us, sitting in his Lexus in the asphalt parking lot, with the heater going full blast. The little onion-covered burgers melted in my mouth. Sean stared at me, exasperated. "Don't you want to fool around?"

"With *you*?" I asked like he had three heads.

"You used to like to."

"That was before."

Sean tossed his empty bag over the back of the seat. "What do you want me to do?"

"Be nice to me."

"I am being nice to you."

"Is it difficult?"

"No."

"Good."

Sean started the car and gave me a look. "Where should we go now?"

"I better get home."

"Okay. You want to do something tomorrow?" he asked.

"Sure," I said, marveling at the turn of events. Sean had come back to me. And I wasn't being a pushover.

CHAPTER

THIRTY-THREE

"Come on, let's go," Sean urged. "You're so lazy." He jabbed my thigh as I lay in bed.

"How did you get up here?"

"Your mom."

I wanted to jump out of bed and grab the Scope, except that I was tenting my undies. What was the protocol here? Should I ask him to turn around? Hell, tease him with it. I jumped out of bed and waltzed to the bathroom, feeling Sean's eyes on me.

"Where are we going?" I asked as I pulled on jeans and a jersey.

"Christmas shopping."

"Good. I need to do that."

Downstairs, Mom insisted on making us cheddar-and-bacon omelets before we left. After setting the bulging egg creations before us, complete with buttered whole-wheat toast, she stood with a mug of hot coffee, watching us eat. She asked Sean annoying questions like what colleges he was considering and whether he had visited any yet. He acted real polite.

The grass in our front yard was crunchy with hard frost as we crossed to Sean's car. "Where should we shop?" Sean asked.

"How about Mall of America?"

"Too many people from school," he said, eyeing me. "Let's go out to Ridgedale." Sean cranked up the radio, and we cruised to the burbs.

Ridgedale is your typical upscale mall decked out for Christmas. Silver and gold balls the size of melons, Wisconsin-cheese wagons fixed with hay and red gingham, piped-in holiday songs. Why did everyone love the phoniness?

Sean knew just where he wanted to go. Ralph Lauren. He grabbed two lambswool sweaters off the sale table, tossing me a forest-green one. "Try this on. It'll look good."

The sale price was still twice what Mom ever paid.

As Sean tried on a charcoal V-neck, his T-shirt slid up, and I saw the fuzzy blond strip of hair on his belly.

"You like it?" he asked when I pulled on the green sweater.

"It's expensive."

"I'll get it for you for Christmas."

"Umm, no."

"David, I can afford it."

He followed me out of the dressing room as I folded the sweater and put it back. "Thanks, anyway," I said. He looked a little hurt. Was I being too hard on him?

Sean knew how to shop, so I followed his lead. In addition to sweaters and a new pair of shoes for him, we bought perfume for our moms and Hawaiian shirts for his dad. Then we went to the food court and scarfed down cheese enchiladas with mouth-burning salsa. The loop on the Christmas music started over again. I made a gagging face at Sean. "Get me outta here."

"Want to go for a run?" he asked.

I looked at my leather shoes. "In loafers?"

"We can swing by your house. My stuff's in the car."

"Hey, Mom," I said, breezing into the house with Sean. She was talking on the phone while folding laundry. "What's up?" she asked, cupping the phone.

"Nothing," I replied.

We pulled on running shorts and T-shirts and then zipped into our thick fleece jackets. "Bye, Mom," I said as we clambered down the steps.

"Where are you going?"

"For a run."

"Will you be here for dinner?"

I looked at Sean, who gave a quick shake to his head as he moved toward the door.

"Doubt it." I followed Sean out.

He drove to the Ford Parkway Bridge on the Minneapolis side. Above the trees to the west, the sun cast long rays of yellow. Sean stretched his hamstrings on a park bench. On the grass next to him, I crouched, thrusting one leg back and then the other, bouncing.

Limbered up, we started off, jogging at first. Crossing the

bridge to St. Paul, we gradually sped up, turning onto the paved path on the far side of the river. A side ache tore into me, but I pushed through it.

We were flying now stride for stride; Sean, ahead of me, bathed in light. I moved up close behind, feeling warmth from him on one side, the sun on the other. I found that sound, the rhythm of his deep breaths, rushing in and out, methodically, like a heart beating.

We glided up the parkway, our strides in tandem. Sunlight pooled on the green lawns in front of the big River Road houses. Scattered leaves, tossed by the wind, landed in window wells and frost-killed gardens, cozying up together for the winter. Our feet clapped the pavement. Flip-step, flip-step, flip-step. Runner's bliss.

At the Lake Street Bridge, Sean turned to complete our loop. The sun fell behind the horizon as we crossed the wide, silent Mississippi. The chill that came with the disappearing sun cooled my hot face.

As we headed up West River Road, Christmas lights started to appear. A massive Norway pine was draped in twinkling blue lights. They must have used a cherry picker to string them all the way to the top. Sean slowed, and we both gazed up at the tree towering above us, its blinking lights going off and on in the darkening sky.

Past Minnehaha Academy we started to ease our pace, first to a jog and then to a walk. My lungs were working hard.

"You're looking good, man," Sean said.

"I'm great if I can just focus on your breathing," I replied.

Sean shook out his legs, and I stretched my haunches. Then he reached into the car and grabbed the cell phone.

"Who you calling?"

"My parents. See if they've left." He dialed and stood waiting. "Mom," he said, "where are you?" I dropped onto the grass.

From his side of the conversation, it sounded like he was getting grilled about what he was doing. But Sean was the master of the evasive answer.

He finally hung up, tossed the phone into the car, and turned to me. "Let's go to my house."

"Your parents going out?"

He nodded. I sat back on the grass, hesitant.

"Come on." He pulled me up by one arm.

I wanted to flop back onto the ground and insist he take me home. But that was not how this was about to end. I knew that.

Inside Sean's huge kitchen, all white marble and dark wood cupboards, I sat on a stool at the counter. Sean handed me a bottle of water as he guzzled one himself. Then he started pulling things out of the refrigerator. "You hungry? This German ham. You gotta taste it." Sean opened deli packages. Then he pulled two thick onion rolls out of a brown bag, sliced them, and slathered them with Dijon mustard.

The ham was cut thin, and we speared big piles of it, making overstuffed sandwiches with Swiss cheese. I chomped into the salty creation, squirting mustard out the sides of my mouth. Sean laughed as he got a liter bottle of tonic water out of the fridge and poured it into two glasses.

"Want some gin?" he asked. He took down a bottle and poured some into his tonic. Why not? I held my glass out.

When we finished our sandwiches, Sean fixed another gin and tonic for himself, but I didn't take one. He put water in the bottle and set it carefully back in the liquor cabinet. "Let's go up to my room," he said, swirling the ice in his drink.

As we took the stairs, two at a time, he sniffed at my armpit and made a face. "Take a shower, man."

Inside his room, Sean cranked up jazz on the radio. We played Game Boys. The gin hit me, and I started to feel light-headed. Sean announced he was taking a shower. He got up and stripped his running clothes off. I pretended to keep playing the Game Boy, but watched his every move. "Don't you need a shower, Dahlgren?"

I looked up. If I went in there, it was all over. He had me again.

"Come on," he urged, bouncing in place.

I tore off my shorts and joined him in the steaming glass stall.

We washed each other everywhere. The hot water, the sight of him, the slippery friction almost took me over the edge. But I held back.

Toweling off in his bedroom, we were still keyed up. He boxed my arm, and I pushed him. He popped me again. "Stop it," I ordered playfully, pushing him down onto the bed, pressing my squeaky-clean body onto his. He resisted and we wrestled. At one point, he flipped on top of me. I struggled to get out from under. He pinned my arms with his knees and rose above me.

To the victor go the spoils. I opened my mouth.

Sean let out little moans, far apart at first and then closer and closer together. His excitement drove me past my ability to control myself and I yanked him down on top of me, clinging to him with one arm, working him with the other. He groaned and arched his back. His breath came harder. I clutched tight. All of a sudden, he flipped us over. My whole body came down on him. He lunged for my lips and kissed me hard. Sean's whole body shuddered as fireworks went heavenward.

I kissed his neck. Sean shoved his fingers over my mouth, rolled off me, and fell back on the pillow. I reached for his shoulder, but he jumped out of bed. "Where you going?" I asked, propping myself up on my elbows.

He disappeared into the bathroom, pulling the door tightly closed behind him.

I knew we were through for now. But wow! He kissed me. Passionately. We had moved into the third dimension. I let my head flop back onto the pillow and finished what Sean paid no mind to.

Ten minutes went by, then fifteen. What was he doing in there? I pulled on some sweats and listened at the door. The shower was running full blast. I pushed open the door. Sean tried to slap it closed, but it was too late. I saw him. Sitting sideways on the toilet, bent over. Crying.

"What's wrong?"

"Get out of here." He wiped at his eyes.

"Sean, what is it?"

He started sobbing again. "God, I can't take this."

I tried to comfort him, but he batted my arms away. "Come on, Sean, that was fantastic. What's so bad?"

"My parents," he said, sobbing. He balled a towel up in his face. "And the team."

Sean kept crying, and I didn't know what to say. I tried to put my arm around him.

"STOP IT!" He shoved me out, closing the door. I stood at his window, waiting, my heart breaking. For him. And for me.

Finally the shower water went off, Sean came out and put on clothes. "I'll drive you home," he said.

I tried to get a conversation started in the car, but Sean wasn't talking. When he stopped in front of my house, I told him about Jim at the Gay Hotline. "Maybe he can help you."

Sean sneered. "Thanks for the advice, Doctor."

"Can I call you?" I asked.

"No."

"Will you call me?"

"Every night. Like lover boys do."

"Don't be an asshole."

"I am an asshole. Didn't you know that?"

I hesitated. "Yeah, I guess." We reached my house.

"You getting out or not?"

So much for happy endings.

CHAPTER

THIRTY-FOUR

Finals week arrived before anyone was ready. Competitive angst hung in the air, weighing us down. My fellow students weren't going to the U of M. They were going east to the Ivy League or Stanford. At least they hoped.

Monday was English. Sean sat hunched over *Siddhartha* before class started, cramming desperately. I bet you fail, I mouthed at the back of his head. And then I imagined shouting out that I loved him. In front of everyone.

There was just one essay question. We had to discuss characterization, using three protagonists from the novels we had read. Afterward, I waited for Sean. I couldn't help myself. He made me mad, but in a way he was pitiful.

Sean was the last to exit and looked bothered. "What's a protagonist?" he asked me.

I did a double take. "The person the book's about."

"Uh-oh."

"Why? What did you answer?"

He shook his head. "This could be bad." He started to walk off down the hall.

"Detweiler's an easy grader," I said, following him. Sean shrugged.

"You want to get a hamburger or something?"

"No, thanks," he replied, cutting down the stairs.

I watched him go. God! This guy.

I woke tired each morning that week, having fallen asleep in my clothes with lamplight shining on my face and a book on my chest. If I had dreams of getting A's, they dimmed as each day went by. In History on Friday, my answer contrasting the French and American revolutions actually began with this sentence: "In the French Revolution, the soldiers spoke French while in the American Revolution, the soldiers spoke English."

When school let out that day, the hallways buzzed with a celebratory mood. However we had done, finals were over. People left quickly, knowing that they would see each other again in a few hours at the dance that night.

As I walked away from Whitman, I wondered what it would be like to go to the dance alone. I didn't expect Sean to call. Or Kick. Or Eddie. I wandered aimlessly around the snowy streets. There on Nicollet was Vintage Flicks. Going inside to browse, I found *My Beautiful Laundrette*, the movie that guy at the gay bookstore had mentioned. That would take care of tonight. Or I could always go over to Grandma's and play cards.

From the parking lot, you could hear the crashing twang of the band's electric guitars. Seventies night. I broke down and walked to school, planning to stay for a few minutes. Inside the gymnasium, geometric shapes in Day-Glo colors hung from the ceiling like celestial objects, transformed by the black lights shining over the crowd. Up on stage, the band was jamming. Dancing pairs, some with white shirts glowing, filled the floor.

I made my way across the room, pretending I had someone to talk to on the other side. Then I saw them. Brenda and Sean. Oh, my God. I couldn't believe he brought her. With his arm around her, no less. The fake.

I escaped to the crepe-papered tables where the PTA was serving lemon bars and chocolate fondue. Searching the room for someone to talk to, I dipped a kiwi slice into the molten chocolate and popped it into my mouth.

I walked over to Jan Freymeyer, from grade-school days.

"Hey, I'm looking for bowling partners," she said, swinging her big frame to the music as her friend Beth pulled her out onto the floor. "Want to go over break?"

I nodded. Sure. Why not? I danced with them for a few minutes and then dropped out.

Not seeing anyone else to talk to, I went to the bathroom. Pushing open the lavatory door, I heard him. "Pssssst . . . David." There he was behind me, checking up and down the hallway to see that we were alone. "Meet me in the parking lot," he whispered in my ear. "Five minutes." He hurried away.

What's this? Did Sean want to work things out with me? Yeah, in a threesome with Brenda.

Sean's motor was running when I got to the lot. "Where we going?" I asked.

"To get cigarettes."

"You don't smoke. Do you?"

"For Brenda."

"Oh, God!"

Sean grabbed my shoulder and gave it a hard squeeze. He drove into the Holiday Station parking lot and jumped out, returning a minute later with a pack of Salems and some candy. "Want a cig?" he asked as he exited the lot and turned up Minnehaha Parkway.

"Where we going?"

Sean didn't answer. He lit a cigarette, drove a mile or so, and turned into one of the empty lakeside parking lots. The overhanging trees made it very dark. Sean flicked the cigarette out the window, looked at me, and then jerked down his zipper.

"What are you doing?" I asked.

"Come on."

"Wait," I said.

He cupped my head and started to shove it down, lifting his hips from the seat.

This was all wrong. I broke free of his grip and shoved his arm away. His eyes flashed at me, and then he started the car.

"Thought I was doing you a favor."

My head slumped down. "Not even close."

I opened the door and climbed out. Sean roared off. At the end of the block, the car stopped abruptly and backed up. He lowered the window on my side. "Get in." I vigorously shook my head, and he floored it.

CHAPTER

THIRTY-FIVE

As I stood next to a snowbank, flushed, watching Sean's taillights recede into the darkness, the cold seeped inside my jacket. The thought of his hand on the back of my head made me shiver. I started walking. Where to? Not home. I didn't want to be alone. Not now.

It was the wind that made the long walk back so cold. But I chose my destiny.

Reaching the school, I stared at the building from across the street. Music drifted through the air as cheery yellow light spilled out over the snow-draped window ledges. It made me lonely.

Then I saw him. Heading to the front door. "Hey," I yelled, waving my arms. "EDDIE!"

He turned. I made a mad dash for him. "Don't go in!" I yelled, charging up the steps.

"Why not?"

I reached the top. "I need to talk to you."

"So, talk." He pulled open the door.

"Wait!"

Eddie turned. "What's wrong, David? You're shaking."

"Stay out here."

"Let's go in where it's warm."

I shook my head. I couldn't say what I had to say inside the school. And truth be told, I didn't want anyone to see me walk in with him.

Eddie wound his scarf around his neck and stuffed his bare hands into his jacket pockets. "So, what is it?" he asked.

The events of the last few months whirled in my head. "Where do I start?"

"Come on."

"Well . . . you see . . ." I stopped.

Eddie started jumping up and down. "I'm freezing, you bonehead. Let's have it."

"Be nice, okay?" I took a deep breath and watched the vapor escape into the night air. Eddie implored me with his eyes. "Okay, okay," I said. "I was out with Sean tonight. I mean, we left the dance together. To get cigarettes."

"Yeah?"

"And on the way back, in the car, something happened."

"What?"

"Well, I mean, we've done stuff before."

"What stuff? Pot?"

"No."

"Coke?"

"No, no. Physical stuff."

"Sex?" Eddie's eyes lit up.

"Well, yeah, sort of." There. I said it.

"Finally," Eddie crowed. "You told me."

"Shhhhh."

"Welcome to the club." He threw his arm around me, friendly-like. "So, what happened with Sean?"

"This time he forced me. Or at least he tried to."

"Ooh, that's hot."

"No, it's not." I sloughed Eddie's arm off me. "It was creepy."

"What did you do?"

"Got out of the car."

Eddie laughed. "That's so Claudette Colbert." My eyes teared up. Eddie's face softened. "Hey. You want to go get french fries or something?"

Sweet. Better than I deserved. "But . . . ," I said, "you were headed for the dance."

"Only in hopes of seeing Tyler Thomas." Eddie hugged his chest. "I'm so in love with him. But it's hopeless."

"Go in. He's there."

"Come with me." Eddie grabbed my hand.

I jerked it away. What did he think?

He stepped back. "What's wrong? You still afraid to be seen with me?"

"Let *me* tell people in my own way, Eddie."

He shook his head. "I never told anyone about you, despite what you think."

"People seem to know."

Eddie shrugged and turned away.

With each second I stood there, the feeling that I was doing the wrong thing grew stronger. Was I a hopeless weakling? Eddie reached the door, turned, and stuck his tongue out.

"Wait," I called. I ran toward him.

He pulled open the heavy wooden door, and the sounds of disco floated out. A respectable cover of Gloria Gaynor. How appropriate. "Hurry!" Eddie said. "I *love* this song."

The gym was still crowded, the dance floor packed. I was keenly aware of being noticed entering with Eddie. "There's Kick." Eddie pointed. "And Mona." They each gave him a big hug.

"Hello, David," Mona said coolly. My eyes met Kick's. She gave me a sad smile. Which sort of killed me. Mona grabbed Kick's hand and pulled her out on the floor.

"Chloe!" Eddie called across the room, waving her over to us. She had dyed her buzz-cut hair like the fur of a leopard. "How fabulous!" Eddie ran his fingers over her head. Then he gestured to me.

"Look who I found lying in a snowbank."

Chloe laughed.

"How did you do that?" I asked, staring at her hair.

"Want me to do yours?" she asked.

"I'd love to see that," Eddie said. "Hey, I'll get us Cokes."

As Eddie walked away, Rick Cutter grabbed his shoulder. "What are you doing here?" he asked in a loud voice. "No faggots."

"How did you get in then?" Eddie replied.

"You little shit." He shoved Eddie.

Eddie shoved him back.

"You want to fight, cocksucker?" Cutter's eyes were smoking.

He pushed Eddie toward the door. Eddie gave ground. Cutter shoved him again and Eddie sat down on the floor.

"I'll fight ya," Chloe said, jumping in front of Eddie. She got her wiry ninety pounds into a crouch. "C'mon, I'll take you on, fuckface." She pumped her arms at Cutter.

He stared at her and started to laugh. "I'm getting out of here before I get AIDS." Cutter purposely pranced to the other side of the dance floor.

Mona and Kick converged on the scene.

"What now?" Eddie asked, still sitting on the floor of the gym.

"Let's jump him," Chloe urged.

Eddie shook his head. "I want to show him I can be here. I want to dance."

"I'll dance with you," Kick offered.

"No. With a guy." He looked at me.

"Me?"

"Yeah, you, weak knees," Chloe said.

C'mon, I was really trying—but did I have to be ready for that? I looked over at Sean against the wall, his arm around Brenda.

The music started up again. "Dancing in the Street." Fear gripped me.

Eddie stood up, looking intently at me.

"Let's all go," I said.

"Okay," he agreed.

The five of us moved through the crowd until we found some space.

Kick, Mona, Chloe, Eddie, and I made a circle of sorts and began to boogie.

The beat revved me up. I put my arms straight up and started clapping. Eddie hooted. The circle merged and converged and then broke apart, until at one point, Eddie and I were on the floor together.

"Awesome," he said. "A guy is dancing with me."

I could feel the eyes on us. Let 'em look. It was done now. I threw my head back. The hard-driving music took hold. I let loose, hair flying, elbows jerking, legs bouncing, not caring, for one moment, not caring what anyone thought. The five of us came back together, rocking as one, in a swirling circle.

When the song ended and we rejoined the milling crowd on the sidelines, everything seemed just the same, except how I felt inside. Proud that I had some guts. But also very exposed.

It was midnight, and the band announced its last song. I was too hot and sweaty to go on and headed for the can. I walked in and drew back. Guys lined the urinals. There was one opening next to Harvey Gersh. I didn't want to pee next to him. But people noticed me just standing there, and I stepped forward.

Harvey gave a start when he saw me. "Hey, Dahlgren," he

called over his shoulder after he'd finished and headed for the door. "Which one of you is the girl?"

I could feel my ears turn red as the bathroom erupted in laughter. But Harvey was gone. Guys were watching me for my reaction as I walked to the sink. I just looked each one in the eye. It was all I could do. It was all I had to do.

CHAPTER

THIRTY-SIX

Saturday night, Mom was out with that guy, Gary, a second time, and I had the house to myself. I invited Eddie over to watch *My Beautiful Laundrette*. He was surprised I had rented it.

Eddie arrived, tossing his chartreuse scarf on the couch like a diva.

"Look at that," he said, laughing at the new zit on the end of my nose. Always the thoughtful one.

"You want hot cocoa?" I asked, putting a bowl of milk in the microwave.

Eddie nodded, and closed his eyes. "I'm so in love. My sweet man, Tyler."

"Your sweet man?"

"Do you know what he said to me?"

" 'Stop looking at my crotch'?" I guessed.

"Nooo. He said my earring was cool."

"Eddie, he's straight."

"Is he?"

"Not in your dreams, I guess."

Eddie sighed. The lovesick fool.

I stirred the cocoa powder into the steaming bowl, dropping in lots of little colored marshmallows. Upstairs in the den, we settled on the floor in front of the TV. "When did you first know?" Eddie asked, sipping from his mug.

"Know what?"

"That you're gay." Eddie snapped his fingers at me. "C'mon, girl, keep up."

"Don't call me 'girl.'"

"So, come on," he said. "When did you first know?"

I leaned back on a pillow next to him. "Eighth grade, I guess." The day was burned into my brain. "Someone brought pictures to music class. Nude close-ups of this woman with her legs spread."

Eddie wrinkled his face. "Ick."

"Tell me about it. But everyone else got horny."

"I knew since I was six," Eddie said.

"Six?"

"That's when Dad started taking me to his gym." Eddie took a deep breath. "I knew I wasn't supposed to be staring at the men in the showers, but I liked to."

"At age six you knew. Wow."

"Well, I knew I was different. That I had to keep it secret."

When he said that, my eyes started to fill up.

"What is it?" Eddie asked.

"I've been hiding for so long." Tears came. I didn't mind Eddie seeing. He knew. He really knew.

"It hurts," he said.

I wiped my eyes and looked up. Eddie had the cocoa cup

tilted against his face. He was totally focused on getting the glob of melted marshmallows into his mouth. Laughing, he asked, "Are you okay?"

"Nooo. Not that you would care."

"Don't get bitchy."

I brushed at my eyes again. "I want people to see me. You know?"

"They will. You're out now. And at the same time part of the secret fraternity."

"What's that?"

"Guys like us. Looking for beauty, entertainment . . . and dick."

"Eddie!"

"It's true."

"Am I in now?"

"We'll work on it." He held up his empty mug. "Is there any more?"

Returning with full cups of cocoa, we started the movie. Eddie curled up under my quilt. It felt so easy to be sprawled on the den floor with him, watching the story of two men falling in love. And when they kissed passionately? First time I saw that on screen. Oh, dear God!

As the movie neared the end, I heard my mother's key in the front door. I jumped up. "Pause it."

"Why?"

"My mom will come in here."

"So?"

"It's a gay movie."

Eddie pushed me out of his line of vision. "I'm sure your mother already knows about you."

"No, she doesn't."

"You should tell her then. I thought you wanted to stop hiding."

"Not right now."

"Shhhhh." He pulled the quilt around himself. "We're missing the end."

Reluctantly, I sat back down to watch. Mom probably wouldn't know the movie anyway.

A minute later she was in the doorway. "Well, hi, Eddie." She stepped into the room. "What are you guys watching?"

"*My Beautiful Laundrette*," Eddie replied.

"Oh. With Daniel Day-Lewis?" she asked.

"Right," Eddie said.

She looked at me as if she were trying to puzzle something out. Here we were, Eddie and I together on the floor; he wrapped in my quilt, watching a film with a gay love story. Not how most guys were spending their first night of vacation.

"I liked that movie," she said, fixing her gaze on me. "It was touching."

And with that, she left.

CHAPTER

THIRTY-SEVEN

Mom spent Sunday afternoon at Grandma's making orange-glaze cookies, *krumkache,* ginger creams, and *lefse.* I tossed myself from one piece of furniture to another. I had to tell her. But I couldn't. What if she had a bad reaction? My mom wouldn't be like that. I hoped.

When she pulled up to the garage, I ran out to help. She had seven tins full of Norwegian Christmas cookies she'd baked. We carried them inside, and she started a pot of coffee. I found the ginger creams and popped one into my mouth. "Fantastic," I said, licking the sweet white frosting from my fingers.

"You and Eddie seem friendly again," she said, getting down her coffee mug.

"Yup."

"I like him. So, what did you two think of *My Beautiful Laundrette?*"

"Good," I said, taking another ginger cream.

"It's an old film. How did you hear about it?"

The bar slipped out of my hand, landing frosting side

down. Should I tell her now? I scooped up the fallen ginger cream and shoved the whole thing into my mouth.

"I heard some guys talking about it," I said through my mouthful. "Sounded good."

"What guys? I'm curious."

I took a big breath. "At a gay bookstore, Mom." She took me in with her eyes as only she could. "I really don't know how to tell you this. So I'm just gonna say it right out."

"I think you just did."

"Okay?"

"David, are you sure? You're so young."

"It's how I feel. I don't think it's going to change." That worried look of hers took hold. "What's wrong?" I asked.

"Nothing."

"Yes, there is."

She studied me, weighing her words. "I love you so much, David. I don't want you to get hurt."

That made my eyes well up. She always got to me with her soft look.

She reached across the table and squeezed my sticky hand. I tried to stop my sobs, but when I saw tears roll down her cheeks, it was all over.

"Oh, David, I think I've always known."

"You have?"

"Yes, somehow." I wiped my eyes on my napkin. "Just little things," she said. "Your sensitivity. But then there was Kick. That threw me off."

"We're just friends."

"You didn't have sex with her?"

I swallowed. The conversation had gone far enough. I needed air. "Isn't it time for us to get a Christmas tree?" I said.

She looked out the window at the dimming light. "It's so cold. Let's go in the morning when it's sunny."

"No. Let's go now."

"All right. You go. And I'll get the ornaments down from the attic."

In the falling snow, the Y's Men's lot on Hiawatha Avenue was the picture of Christmas. Rows of conifers stood full and green in the gathering snow, waiting to be chosen. The cool minty smell of pine filled my lungs as I put my face in the tree boughs. And there it was. A balsam with branches still lashed tight to its trunk. Why hadn't anyone unbound the poor tree?

I released its cramped branches and looked it over. This one will do fine, I thought. So what if there was a gap on one side. We could put that toward the back. I paid for the tree and walked it to the car, exhilarated by the thought that I was out to my mother. And things were okay.

That's when I saw him. What was he doing here? He lived miles away. I ducked behind the fender, but he spied me.

"David!" he yelled, running my way. I stood waiting. "Could you give me a lift? Brenda and I just broke up. She wouldn't give me a ride home."

I shrugged. "Sure. Get in."

Sean slipped inside the car while I tied the balsam to the roof. The last moments of twilight were giving way.

"What happened with Brenda?" I asked as we started off.

"She was always ragging. I wasn't romantic enough. I didn't pay enough attention to her. I'm glad it's over."

We came to a stop at a red light. Sean looked all around like he was trying to spot someone. He pulled his stocking cap down over his head so you could barely see his face.

"Are you cold?" I asked, turning onto a side street leading to his house. Then it hit me. I stopped dead in the road. "You're afraid to be seen with me." Sean didn't look up. "Aren't you?"

A car pulled up behind me and honked. "David, you're holding up traffic."

"I don't believe this," I said. "You better get out." The car honked again, and I pulled over.

"David, please, it's cold. Take me home."

"No. If that's how you feel, you shouldn't take a ride from me." I hit the automatic unlock. FLAMP. The locks flew open. I stared at him, waiting. "You're only ten blocks away."

He stared at me. "Don't be a jerk."

"You're the jerk." I grabbed his hat and pulled it off his head. "You're ashamed of me. You shit."

He grabbed his hat back and pulled it on. "I don't want a reputation."

"Oh, God, stop the bull! What are you afraid of?"

"I'm not afraid."

My eyes held his. "Well, then? We could really have something."

Sean slumped in the bucket seat. "I wish I could."

"Why can't you?"

"I'm not going to be part of your faggy life."

"What *are* you going to do? Hang with Parker? Make out with girls?" I reached out and rubbed his shoulder.

"Forget it." He pulled away. "Let's go."

"This is our last chance."

"As if we ever had one."

I stared out at the icicles hanging off the peaked roof of the house across from me. "We did. That's the sad part."

Sean pulled the hat down to just below his eyebrows.

I drove him home anyway.

"Thanks," he said, getting out and slamming the door.

I gave the car some gas, watching him get smaller and smaller in the rearview mirror. The first love affair of my life. Over. And was I changed for it? Like the sun during a solar eclipse.

Picking through a box of red, blue, and gold ornaments, deciding which ones to hang in the front of the tree, I looked over at Mom. "What do you want for Christmas?"

"Should I say A's and B's on your report card?"

"You better pick something money can buy. Finals were hard. Except for English. That one I nailed. Unlike Sean—who didn't know what a protagonist was."

"Really?"

"Can you believe that?"

"How is Sean?"

"I don't know."

"Can I ask you something? Is he gay too?"

"Mom!" Details about Sean were off-limits right now.

"I'm just curious if you have gay friends."

"Well, Eddie's obvious. But that's all I'm saying, okay?"

She looked up from where she was bent over unwrapping tinsel. "Yeah, that's okay." She gave me a hug and began draping the tree in the silver icicles. "Aren't these festive?"

They were. Mom handed the tinsel to me, went in the kitchen, and fixed us a plate of ginger creams and *krumkache*. Together we finished it off, never having dinner. The tree looked amazing when we were done. I went to bed tired, but feeling good. Better than I'd felt in a long time, really.

Maybe it was the sugar rush.

CHAPTER

THIRTY-EIGHT

"There's a gay beach in Minneapolis?" I bit into Rudolphs bacon cheeseburger and looked across the restaurant booth at Eddie.

"Yeah, Lake Calhoun. And it's hot."

"I used to jog by there Saturday mornings. Never saw it."

"No one's there in the morning." Eddie shook his head at me.

Then I noticed this dark-haired guy with a mustache coming toward us; Eddie kicked me under the table. "That's my type," he whispered.

"Isn't it everyone's?"

I thought Eddie was going to get up and tackle him.

"How's Kick?" I asked, to distract him.

"Fine. Everyone's going over there tomorrow. Why don't you come?"

"I can't."

"Why not?"

"I have to give her space."

"She's over you."

"Yeah?"

"You think you're so unforgettable? She met somebody else."

"She did?" That was fast.

"You're not jealous, are you?"

"Maybe a little."

"Why? Don't you want to meet a guy?"

I checked the tables around us to make sure no one was listening. "Yeah," I said.

"Good. We can look for boyfriends together. There's a gay dance at the U on New Year's Eve. Want to go?"

The idea sounded intriguing. Handsome college guys. No connection to Whitman.

"Okay. I'm in." I grabbed a fry and stirred it in ketchup. "And if I meet someone"—I sucked the fry into my mouth— "who knows what might happen?"

"Maybe he'll be as horny as Sean. But more into you."

That sounded good.

I rang the chimes at Kick's house and stood waiting in the wintry night.

Kick pulled open the door and looked out. I smiled sheepishly. "Hope this is all right. Eddie said I should come."

"It's fine." She held open the door. I saw her parents reading in the living room.

"You look good," I said. "I like the pants."

"Oh, these?" She ran her hands up and down the black velvet legs. "They're fun, aren't they?"

I whispered. "How are things with your parents? Still guarding you?"

"Of course." She leaned in toward me, and I could smell her perfume. "They bugged my phone."

"No, really?"

"That's what Zach said."

"Zach?"

"From ski club."

"So you and Zach are together now."

"I don't know." Kick shrugged. "He seems to really like me. Go on upstairs. Eddie and Mona are in the den. I'll get munchies."

"Let me help," I offered.

"No, I can manage."

I lingered for a moment, studying her. "You sure?"

"Yes." We were feeling our way now. I headed up the soft carpeted stairs two at a time and said hi to Eddie and Mona.

A moment later, Kick struggled through the doorway, juggling sodas, two bags of chips, and a plastic tub of onion dip. "Sorry," she said, laughing as the cans dropped to the floor like torpedoes. "Still working on my hostess skills."

Eddie picked up a can and handed it to Mona. "So how's your boyfriend?" he asked her. "Does he like his halfway house?"

Mona chortled. "Shut up. He was only held for questioning."

I grabbed a soda and popped the top.

"You caused quite a stir the other night," Kick said to me, sitting down.

"What do you mean?"

"I shouldn't tell you this," Kick said.

"You have to now."

"Your cross-country buddies were freaked out when they saw you dancing with Eddie."

My chest tightened. "What did they say?"

"Parker, mainly. Said he didn't want you on the team."

"They can't do that," Eddie said. "We'll sue."

"I bet he never says that to your face," Kick said.

"But he thinks it."

"So what if he does?"

I didn't have a good answer for that. But I wasn't quitting.

After we polished off the snacks, our next stop was the movies. We got dressed in our heavy winter coats. "Look!" Kick exclaimed when we stepped out into the clear, cold night. "Moon shadows."

There the four of us were, in silhouette, next to the drifts of snow. "Make an angel," Eddie dared us. Mona and Kick shook their heads and hurried down to the car.

"If you go first," I said.

Eddie flumped onto his back in the fresh snow and started moving his arms and legs. He looked up at me standing over him. White powder clung to his hair and ears. "Come on, buddy."

I jumped, doing a half twist in the air and

back next to him. We stared up at the rising m

"Do you think it was just by accident?" E

etly, pondering the thought. "That you and I g

in grade school?"

"What do you mean?"

"Maybe, without knowing it, gay boys find

"Could be," I said. "It's a nice thing if it's tr

"They're out there right now," Eddie said

forts together. Future queers of America."

I laughed.

Kick's voice rang through the night air. '

guys."

Eddie jumped to his feet and started brush

I extended my arm toward him. He grabbed m

back for leverage, and hoisted me out of the sn

"Hurry up!" Mona shouted.

Eddie ran for the car. I lingered for a mome

the angels we had left in the snow. "Keep an ey

under my breath and raced off to join my frien

I grabbed a soda and popped the top.

"You caused quite a stir the other night," Kick said to me, sitting down.

"What do you mean?"

"I shouldn't tell you this," Kick said.

"You have to now."

"Your cross-country buddies were freaked out when they saw you dancing with Eddie."

My chest tightened. "What did they say?"

"Parker, mainly. Said he didn't want you on the team."

"They can't do that," Eddie said. "We'll sue."

"I bet he never says that to your face," Kick said.

"But he thinks it."

"So what if he does?"

I didn't have a good answer for that. But I wasn't quitting.

After we polished off the snacks, our next stop was the movies. We got dressed in our heavy winter coats. "Look!" Kick exclaimed when we stepped out into the clear, cold night. "Moon shadows."

There the four of us were, in silhouette, next to the drifts of snow. "Make an angel," Eddie dared us. Mona and Kick shook their heads and hurried down to the car.

"If you go first," I said.

Eddie flumped onto his back in the fresh snow and started moving his arms and legs. He looked up at me standing over him. White powder clung to his hair and ears. "Come on, buddy."

I jumped, doing a half twist in the air and landing on my back next to him. We stared up at the rising moon.

"Do you think it was just by accident?" Eddie asked quietly, pondering the thought. "That you and I got together back in grade school?"

"What do you mean?"

"Maybe, without knowing it, gay boys find each other."

"Could be," I said. "It's a nice thing if it's true."

"They're out there right now," Eddie said. "Making tree forts together. Future queers of America."

I laughed.

Kick's voice rang through the night air. "Come on, you guys."

Eddie jumped to his feet and started brushing himself off. I extended my arm toward him. He grabbed my hand, leaned back for leverage, and hoisted me out of the snowbank.

"Hurry up!" Mona shouted.

Eddie ran for the car. I lingered for a moment and gazed at the angels we had left in the snow. "Keep an eye on us," I said under my breath and raced off to join my friends.